THE NIGHT DREDES

Shayna Grissom

CONTENTS

Helicant

Another day of knee-aching, backbreaking work. Her skin practically flayed from bird-like bones, peeling around the brush as she scrubbed the cobblestone floor. Lye is a necessary unkindness. Helicant knew that better than anyone. Sometimes, in her dreams, she could still smell the sickly sweet odor, like rancid bacon rations dissolving in a pool of alkaline corruption.

Today will be the day...

It was a mantra of sorts for the matriarch of Sallows Hall, for she carried an unfathomable burden.

Everything she did, she did for the girl. Destiny was all that was left of Helicant's wretched old soul. What little goodness and compassion she had, she pushed it from her womb, tearing herself apart to keep it alive. Her child. A beautiful, brilliant girl that was capable of so much if she only had the gumption and the opportunity.

The bristles on her scrub brush rasped against the stones as Helicant worked her way around the cast iron oven in the corner, as well as the wooden worktable in the center of the kitchen. The stones glistened momentarily before wicking the moisture away to places unknown.

Today will be the day...

But she had to finish cleaning. If she didn't, Destiny would come downstairs and try to take the work from her. Helicant had learned through trial and error that if she didn't finish the floors of the kitchen before the finch flew at the window, that Destiny would come and yank the brush from her pruned hands and finish the kitchen herself. On the eve of her wedding of all times!

Everyone knew that lye-burned hands could not be properly held in matrimony.

That boy, Daniel, would need to grow a spine if this was ever going to work. Helicant wasn't concerned with his excess flesh as his parents were. It was baby fat that would be trimmed with time and hard work, and Sallows Hall was nothing but hard work.

She recently closed the east wing—the once great house of the island housed had several dozen rooms—but these days their clan's numbers had dwindled to eleven individuals. The entire population of their island could live in the great house and its populace go months without encountering one another.

Yet somewhere between family disputes and the craving for space, the family broke away from the mansion and made their own home-steads. This suited Helicant, for she disliked people on most days, but it wasn't good for her daughter. Loneliness is the true mother of monsters.

The girl had been isolated for too long with only an old woman for company. In the shadow of so many expectations, her daughter had grown so timid and fearful. Alone in the kitchen, Helicant laughed at the irony.

Imagine someone being born of her ilk having anything to fear.

Marriage would suit Destiny in ways it never suited Helicant. Her daughter would grow stronger, more self-assured. She had to. She had no other choice.

Stepping out the back porch, Helicant dumped the murky gray water into the lawn and set the bucket on the basement steps. Sighing, she wiped her hands on her apron. She still needed to light the stove, sweep, dust, and dress for the party. Her sisters would be here any minute to begin cooking. The notion set her worn, flat teeth on edge.

All the pots and pans had been cleaned in preparation for the event. There would be a feast followed by the proposal. Absently, she rotated the ring around her finger. It was a great cushion cut ruby, surrounded by diamonds. But its weight grew heavier with each passing day.

It marked her as the direct descendant of Nathaniel Sallows, the founder of their island and leader of their mission.

By right, it belonged to Destiny. It was Helicant's hope that with a partner by her side, her daughter might lead the family into the future. The rosebud on the vine had to bloom at some point.

Her back recoiled from the hunched position she kept so long, and her knees sang with reprieve as she fell into the chair beside the worktable. Just a little rest before the day began. The heavy folds of her eyelids sank lower with each blink like a pendulum.

Her mind drifting, Helicant's last fleeting thoughts were on the floor. Within the dips and demarcations of the dry cobblestone, tidepools of soapy water rose seemingly from the stone itself. That wouldn't do. Water must evaporate, not concentrate. This place had no idea how time or nature worked.

Today had to be the day. Helicant didn't think she could keep this up for much longer.

Destiny

Why must marriage be so... Depressing?

Destiny stared at the length of the gown. Sifting beneath the handmade lace overlay rubbing the silky fabric between two fingers. It was luxurious and unlike the hemp-woven materials they usually wore.

This fabric must've been imported or repurposed from a time long before her family came to live in this awful place. Abandoning the wedding gown lingering in the wardrobe, she assessed the overcast sky out the window.

As far back as she could remember, the days were shrouded in murky, storm cloud-filtered light, and their nights screened with a soupy fog. The birds that frequented the forest never took to the sky, and the wild hares that Drew caught in his snares never grazed on the lawn.

Even the animals hated this place.

A smattering of rose red drew her focus. The rose vines she and her papa planted when Destiny was a child. The only color outside of the muted overcast hues were the roses she cultivated and the wild dyes Aunt Coral doused on Destiny's clothing.

While everyone else on the island was content with browns and cremes. She wanted bright, happy colors. Indigos and berry-crushed blues. Pastel reds and greens so bright her mother cringed at her "tacky" designs.

Though her mother would never wear Destiny's designs, Helicant never criticized them. If anything, her mother praised her for her uniqueness. "You have more spirit than all the people on this island combined," Helicant often said.

Destiny didn't know if that was true, for she scarcely knew the others. She and her cousin Abigail were close once, but they all sought distance from her when the night terrors started. Maybe it was her who pushed them away, not wanting to burden her family with lessening opinions and discomfort.

Abigail was her designated bride's maid for the ceremony. The whole family would come to witness the proposal—or sheer humiliation—Destiny was certain it would be the latter. Poor Daniel. She wished she could instill it in his mind, the knowledge that her problems had nothing to do with him.

It was early afternoon, and Abigail still wasn't there. Turning to eye the dress again, she determined there would be no way to put it on herself. It buttoned up the back, and the fit around the waist would be impossible without a corset. Her stomach bobbed at the thought of wearing one of those.

Destiny swore that her mother lived in the things, but Helicant never stressed that she should wear them, so she didn't. In fact, she didn't even know how to lace a corset properly. Without guidance or assistance on the matter, there was no point in trying. Might as well avoid the problem until the last possible moment.

Just outside her door was the long, winding corridor identical to the dozens of other hallways in Sallows Hall. Holding her breath, Destiny opened her door to check for her clues before stepping out. The floor was bare, and her dolls still hung on the doorknobs. Her little tells on which way led to the grand staircase in the center of the home.

She cringed every time she had to navigate through the house. Even after her mother closed off the east wing, there were still plenty of ways to get lost. Three flights and a left turn followed by an immediate right turn. Third door to the right.

There were six stories, not counting the basement, and Destiny avoided most of them.

Pink doll, blue doll, and lastly, the brown doll that hung from the doors of empty rooms, all leading her to the stairs. Destiny resorted to rolling up the runner in her hallway and throwing it in one of the unused rooms to prevent her from mistaking her hallway for one of the others to her mother's protest.

"Why can't we leave the carpet alone?" Her mother asked after several attempts to roll the carpet back out.

"In the dream I'm running through hallways with carpet," Destiny explained. "If this hallway doesn't have a carpet, it's not the corridor in my dream."

Her mother wanted to argue against it, but ultimately, it came down to Destiny feeling safe in her own home. Helicant wouldn't choose a carpet over her daughter's peace of mind.

"I suppose it will make sweeping easier," her mother conceded.

It hurt sometimes, looking back on things. Her heart would ache from the melancholy of it all. Helicant was too old to be managing a daughter who still behaved like a child. All her little dolls and coping mechanisms were dutifully noted and upheld by the matron.

Mother drew the line at the twine Destiny tied and looped around the doors and to the bannisters. That, Helicant said, was a hazard to an old woman's health. The dolls and rug were a compromise.

"Creativity is the key to raising children," Helicant would say, despite only ever having the one. "That and a strong constitution."

Descending the grand staircase was a workout for someone in their twenties, how Mother managed to make it to the fifth floor might have also been due to the old woman's unnatural resilience. She begged and pleaded with her mother to move her bedroom closer, but Helicant refused. All her things were up there.

Navigating through the reception room, Destiny passed through the entryway to finally push open the double doors of the kitchen.

Coming to a clumsy halt, Destiny found her mother fast asleep while sitting up. The old woman's hands were gnarled from decades of arthritis. Red and inflamed, her skin was scaly and raw. Blisters had popped, and the skin peeled in dry curls. Stubborn old hag, she should've let Destiny help.

A mixture of anger over her mother's exertion and nerves over the day's events took its toll. She struggled to breathe as her ribs closed in on her lungs, and her diaphragm heaved on its own accord. A tidal wave of dizziness threatened to pull her under. Leaning against the doorway, standing, and breathing were all she could do.

To make matters worse, a bird flew at the window.

She saw it diving towards the pane of glass like a wayward stone. Willing it to veer away from the house did nothing. Its poor little body slapped against the window hard enough to fracture the glass, leaving a bright smear of blood in its wake.

Destiny'd had enough of the day, and it was only morning.

Closing her eyes, a single, green, bloodshot eye emerged from the dark. Jerking from left to right, it searched for her. He was always searching for her.

Please, Destiny, open the door…

She didn't always dream of him. Sometimes, she'd sit in a field of tall yellow flowers she didn't recognize in a place unknown to her. The cozy warmth of the sun on her face and birds a shade of incredible blue flew overhead. Destiny didn't always dream of him, but he always found her.

It wasn't his green eye or the horrors of his room that hurt so much as the unrelenting guilt in her heart that never ceased. Why did she harbor so much guilt for the creature?

Relief came as footsteps on the gravel outside. Setting aside the night terrors, Destiny focused instead on the muttering old woman outside. Rushing out the backdoor with a smile, she had to stop her aunt Sophie before it was too late.

"Shh," she urged.

Sophie had braided her soft, greying hair into a single French braid and was wearing a housedress lined with holes and patches, suggesting she was here to work. Sophie's blue eyes hardened while waiting for an explanation.

"Mother fell asleep in the kitchen."

Her aunt rolled her eyes and dropped a bucket of vegetables on the ground. "She's overdone it, hasn't she?"

"I told her I could help, but she wouldn't let me."

"Not on your special day," Sophie agreed, and the urge to vomit nearly had her. "I would have come much sooner if she would let me. Beth, myself, and Coral would have done it, but—"

"I know how she is."

Maybe Destiny didn't know half as well as her aunts, but Helicant's stubbornness was as clear as the unmoving stars in the sky. Her mother still considered herself the leader of the island even when there wasn't much left to lead. Helicant expected the same from Destiny, but she didn't see why the likes of Sophie, Beth or anyone else needed her to boss them around. They managed quite well for themselves, even in their advanced years.

In Destiny's estimation, it was her and her mother that lived by the good graces of their family. The others did all the work, lived in the small houses, and she benefited from it all. What did they need her for?

All this fuss over some silly old ring and a promise long forgotten by the rest of the world.

A smile formed on Sophie's waxen face. "Well, I need to make another trip to the cottage anyway. Want to come with?"

Destiny smiled and nodded. She loved Sophie's cottage even if it was where her night terrors came from. Together, they rounded the corner of the mansion but stopped short at the stone hedge wall. She cried out and bit her knuckles. Nothing beautiful, nothing pure or loved, could survive this place.

Her roses...

The roses weren't just trampled. They were ripped to shreds. Rose petals scattered on the ground like blood. Something had torn them down. It had to be recent as they were intact not even a half hour ago.

"What happened?" Sophie gasped.

Destiny couldn't speak; she could only fall to her knees on the damp grass and touch a sad, broken branch. She shouldn't be so upset over some foliage, but she truly was on the verge of tears. This was the closest to a pet Destiny had ever had. Her only friend when her cousins found reasons to exclude her from the games and sleepovers.

Sophie said nothing for a moment. Destiny felt a hand on her shoulder. "Your father helped you plant these here, I know."

Tears sprung from her eyes. She wiped them away sloppily with the sleeve of her oversized coat.

"I tried planting them on the trellis at the maze entrance, you see, and they just would not grow right. No matter how much light or good soil they had, I could never get them to bloom."

"Father said the trellis was too confining, and the reason the roses couldn't grow was because they didn't have enough room. So, he helped me plant them along this wall. I could always look at them on rainy days from outside my bedroom window. He got sick after that."

Sophie listened with an air of gravity. In some ways, Aunt Sophie reminded Destiny of her mother. A softer, more yielding version that understood sentimentality one could find in unimportant things.

Her aunt embraced her in a full, warm hug before they resumed their trek to Sophie's cottage, leaving behind the tattered rose bugs and heavy pawprints on the lawn.

The old cottage was a stone and thatched creation that perched high on the wind-battled cliffs. Surrounded by the wildflowers Sophie cultivated along with a little vegetable garden sectioned off by a picket fence gnawed at by years of winds and ocean spray. Rocks adorned the soggy roof to prevent the winds from whisking Sophie's roof away, but they weren't entirely successful.

Uncle Carl, the established maintenance man, was never out of work.

He was soon to be her father-in-law, and Destiny couldn't help but wonder if there wasn't a larger strategy at work. If Carl and his family moved into Sallows Hall, there would be three men and two women added to their ranks.

Preserving the mansion was always a priority until someone's roof was spirited away, but Daniel and his younger brother Joesph would be more readily available for minor tasks. Mother knew how fond she was of Abigail, and she couldn't help but feel like her favorite cousin was the lure in a trap.

Wrapping her arms around herself did little against the icy pelt of wind. The off-beat path wasn't an easy one, but it was worth it. If she had a choice, Destiny would've preferred living in the cottage over the mansion.

No winding hallways and endless cleaning. That way, she'd only ever get lost in her dreams and wake content beside a crackling fire.

There'd be no evil green eye waiting for her.

Destiny inhaled deeply. The gods had to be real; otherwise, why make such places if no one were to appreciate them? She believed in gods the way she believed in sea creatures like whales and seals; they existed, but they'd long abandoned the island just as the rest of the world had done.

"Why don't we just leave?" Destiny asked.

Boats were another topic in the library. Well established, there were many books on how to craft a ship. Unlike the toilets and their strange, unusable plumbing, ships had to work; otherwise, there wouldn't be several books on the subject. So why not build one and sail to a place with people?

"This is our home," Sophie said. "Sallows were charged with protecting the world from the monsters on this island."

Destiny rolled her eyes. "You don't really believe in all that nonsense, do you?"

"Nathanial Sallows did."

"Yeah, but that was like a thousand years ago."

Sophie giggled. "It was nearly four hundred years ago."

"Just stick a note on the door of the basement saying, 'do not open' and leave."

The smile was gone, leaving a sad, old expression. "I'm afraid that if we leave, we will wash ashore to a new and frightening world. One we'd arrive to without a single penny."

Destiny understood this well enough. Her family would go from being owners of an island, decreed by the king himself, to one of many impoverished families.

"It can't be that different," she argued despite knowing the logic. "I mean, Coral makes my clothes. Edward is a doctor and Beth a Naturalist. There would be work, and we still have lots of gold and gems stashed away in the chests."

"Do you think your mother could survive such a journey?"

Of course she would bring Mother into it.

Destiny cast her eyes downward in defeat. Sophie took her hand and said, "We don't know what the future will bring. Maybe when all of us old folks have gone, you and Daniel can strike out on your own."

Destiny forced a smile, and Sophie gave her a gentle nod before they went into the cottage. Once inside, Destiny's lungs lurched and sent her coughing. Dust and soot scattered and obscured the daylight streaming from the windows. Sophie's face scrunched up as she scowled at the state of her house. There were cobwebs in every corner and an inch of dust layering everything.

"I just dusted this morning, for goodness sake!"

Sophie's little tantrum was comical. Destiny had to stifle a giggle. Her aunt's eyesight must've been going. Under the dust was an open book on every flat surface as though she walked through the house reading a page at a time. It was a bit of a mess, but an inhabited mess. The chaos of a small home filled with books and treasures. There was a map of the island hanging up on the wall and the original blueprints of Sallows Hall.

Destiny noticed that dust covered the inside of the fireplace. How could that much dust accumulate on Sophie's only source for heat? Following her aunt into her bedroom, Sophie let out a gasp as the formal dress that hung on the armoire was also caked in a gray shroud.

"You just set this out, yeah?" Destiny asked.

"Right before I came," Sophie was on the verge of tears. "Helicant will be so cross if I don't wear something appropriate for the event."

Destiny could hear the fear in her aunt's voice and didn't quite understand the source of power her mother had on everyone else. Mother would understand. She might be gruff, but Helicant wasn't as unforgiving as all that.

A gust of wind must have pushed through the chimney, covering the house while Sophie was gone. She couldn't control that.

"It will be okay. I bet Beth has an extra garment."

Sophie nodded, but her eyes were still fixed on the dress.

"She's probably on her way up to the house now, I bet we can borrow a dress and mother will be none the wiser."

Destiny helped Sophie leave the bedroom and guided her into the living room as if her aunt were in a daze. "I just don't understand."

"It's probably something with your chimney. I'll ask Uncle Carl to look at it."

"Yes..." Sophie said, dusting off a small, leather-bound diary. "It must be."

As Sophie wandered out the door, Destiny picked up the single item her aunt bothered to dust before leaving. It was Nathanial's diary. Her fingers trembled across the leather-bound journal in anticipation of its contents.

Everyone thought it was the source of her nightmare, but Destiny knew better. She had the dream long before she read the book. No one understood that, so they just ignored what they couldn't explain.

The handwritten pages still smelled like the pitch-black ink that stained the pages. Destiny thumbed through the diary and looked at the page labeled The Green-Eyed Monster. She was about to read it when she heard Sophie call, "Destiny, are you coming?"

Absently, Destiny slipped the book into her coat and thought no more of it.

She only hoped that they would reach Beth before she wandered into the house to wake up Mother. Unlike her twin, Beth was prone to idle chatting and gossip. Destiny never minded it and thought it was funny, but sometimes her topics veered on carelessness.

"We should try to beat Beth to the house," she said, hurrying along.

Beth

Beth tromped through the off-beaten path that wound up the hill towards her sister's mansion. Her long dress was hot and clung to her skin, and it wasn't even midday yet. Her wide-brim hat did little to offset the heat. Halfway up the hill, she turned to see her husband and her son lagging.

"Hurry up," she urged. "I'm supposed to be there already. Helicant hates it when people are late."

Her husband ignored her as he always did, his eyes squinting in the direction of the mansion. It was her son, Drew, who retorted. "Mother, she doesn't mind if you're late just as long as you are quiet."

Beth pursed her lips. She could feel her cheeks glowing. How dare he be so rude to her? "Edward, are you really going to let him talk to me like that?"

Her husband gave a nod and looked at their son. "As long as you live under my roof, you'll not speak to your mother that way."

Drew's pale skin contrasted with the few ruddy freckles across his nose and cheeks. He was a tall young man with a thick head full of auburn hair. He was handsome like his father but took more of her traits than Beth wanted to admit.

Her son sized up his father. "Why? You do it all the time."

Before he walked away, casual as ever. Beth could only stand there as their son walked up the hill right past her and on to the mansion. What had gotten into that boy? The older he got, the more defiant and ruder he became. It wasn't until Edward caught up with her that Beth rationalized her son's behavior.

"He's just upset that Helicant wouldn't so much as consider him for Destiny."

Edward said nothing. She knew he agreed with her because it was the only reason for Drew to act so callously. They had raised the boy well despite their lower status on the island. Edward deserved a bigger house, being that he was the only doctor on the island, but they made do with what they had.

She linked her arm through his. Edward considered her arm for a moment but accepted the gesture. "Helicant will see soon enough. Daniel isn't the right match for Destiny, and she has that peculiar aversion..."

"His eyes," Edward corrected. "Destiny is afraid of green eyes. It's a phobia. Some people develop them over birds or even leaving their house. Dreadful condition, but it can be overcome with enough time and patience."

Beth's mother had the bird phobia—Helicant had told her as much. Their mother would scream and refuse to leave the house, the pheasants terrorized her so. It wasn't a rational fear but also one that couldn't be dissuaded. The body would react before the mind could tell it otherwise.

"How sad," Beth said.

"She read that damned book in Sophie's house—Nathaniel's diary. Ever since she's had night terrors about a creature with green eyes hiding somewhere within the house."

Beth truly felt sorry for her niece. She had a night terror once. It was the worst experience of her life. She dreamt she couldn't speak, and when she looked down, her jaw was waggling about on her lap. Still made her shudder with revulsion to this day.

"The sedatives didn't help?"

"No, the night terrors still came, only she couldn't wake up from them."

Beth shivered at the thought of being trapped in anything depicted in one of Sophie's books. "Have they at least stopped? Her night terrors?"

Edward shook his head. "I don't think they have."

"Things would be better for everyone if Destiny married Drew," Beth said. "Drew has blue eyes, for one. He's strong and handy, just like you are. Drew is a skilled hunter, even in the dead of winter. We could all move into Sallows Hall. With the four of us, the home would be easier to maintain."

He said nothing, but that didn't mean he disagreed. Beth decided to move the conversation to something he was more comfortable with. A doctor always had part of his mind on work. "Oh, and I'll have those opiates derived for you soon."

Edward's bushy, dark brows raised in surprise. As he had gotten older, the folds of his eyelids grew heavy, but he was still just as dashing in his older years as he was as a young man. Maybe even more so.

Beth nodded. "I finally found that distilling equipment that was missing. They were just where I had left them. I must have looked over them a dozen times, but I distilled the pods."

"That's wonderful," Edward said. "Never know when we need painkillers."

"Let's hope they will not come to use any time soon. I'm still at a loss for what happened to the last vial."

Edward once again fell into a stoic silence. Beth knew he knew, and she wanted answers. As the only botanist without an understudy, she kept an inventory of every medicine she created on the island. Edward and his poor excuse for an understudy were the only two who knew how to do injections.

"You know you can tell me anything."

Her husband stopped walking. "As a doctor, there are certain things I must keep confidential, even from my own wife."

She knew it!

After months of hounding him, of checking Drew's arms without his knowledge, Beth knew the last vial of morphine had to have been used by Edward for something. But what? Who needed to use an entire bottle?

"What of your only pharmacist?" Beth asked. "How am I to provide such drugs without knowing who consumes such quantities and why? That was enough doses to kill three men. How am I to forego my own conscience?"

At this, Edward relented. "The patient is being carefully monitored."

"By who?" Beth asked. "By you? Not possible. Just last week, you were doing work on the mansion."

"Abigail has been my understudy for many years," Edward reminded.

That was what Beth was afraid of. She pursed her lips and walked away from her husband before she could say something she'd regret as she had done so often with Edward. Anger accumulated in her throat like hot bile, and before she could stop herself, she called back to her husband.

"Just be sure the little trollop isn't using it herself."

Edward said nothing. Beth could feel his angry, squinty eyes on her back as she pushed herself up that hill. It would probably be the last conversation they would have for the rest of the day—perhaps even the week, but it was worth it.

ABIGAIL

Abigail couldn't wait for her family any longer. By the time they got to the mansion, the party would be half over. It was Daniel's wedding! Of all things to be late to...

Standing on a stool in the middle of their earth-floor cottage, Daniel was wearing a black suit made of hemp cloth as Mother pulled out the fitting pins. The weave was the tightest her mother had loomed yet, but she'd already seen Destiny's gown, and compared to that, Daniel would look like he was wearing a dishtowel.

She hated the subtle jabs towards her brother's size. Rather than allow Abigail to steal the velvet curtains from the mansion, their mother insisted on making the scratchy hemp cloth so as not to offend her royal crankiness.

"Oh, for Heaven's sake, Abigail!" Coral shouted. "Carl, don't just stand there..."

Abigail looked back for a moment and laughed, leaving the front door of their hovel open. Her father's balding head reflected in the sunlight. He wouldn't pursue her. He seldom took issue with anything his children did. She took to a full sprint down the dirt road that wound up the hillside to the great bastard of a house. The hazy fog of the morning was retreating to the forest, fully exposing the steepness of the hillside.

It was good to be free.

She reached the house, sweaty and winded. Her dress was caked with dirt around the hem, but Abigail didn't care. She and Destiny were nearly the same size, and her cousin would let her borrow something. Abigail's mother was too busy fussing over Daniel's suit and the dress for Destiny to even consider making her own daughter a dress.

Pulling open the arched double doors, Abigail made herself at home. When she wasn't working for the doctor, she helped Helicant with laundry or yard work. The stone-tiled entryway echoed her footsteps. Abigail strained to listen for the sounds of life, but the house felt as though it had been abandoned for ages. Sallows Hall was still and lifeless, as if immune to the numerous souls that made it their life's work to maintain it.

She climbed up three flights of stairs and went down the west wing to find Destiny's room empty.

The little dolls rag dolls hung from the doorknobs, staring at her without faces. A chill rushed up her spine as they watched her pass.

She checked the west wing on the fifth floor. Helicant's room was also empty. Abigail wouldn't fully step into her royal crankiness's room, just enough to see she wasn't there.

Abigail anticipated the house to be full of people now.

Today was a big ordeal, and Helicant was no spring chicken. Had she fallen, leaving Destiny to run to fetch Edward? Did Destiny have an episode so debilitating that they needed to see the doctor together? Her mother would be devastated if the wedding was cancelled. It was understood that Daniel's feelings on the subject were secondary to their mother's. As for Daniel, well, he was fully resigned to rejection.

The large bed had a wolf pelt draped across the entire bed. Its glass eyes faded, but the teeth appeared sharp as ever. Along the headboard was the depiction of a fox on a hill being chased by wolves. There was a story about it, some analogy for how the Sallows came to be on this island, but Abigail preferred the here and now.

Helicant's vanity was lined with bottles and creams—things she had either made herself or had Beth concoct for her. Abigail noted the black dress resting across the bed. It seemed the matron had been preparing before their disappearance.

The drawing room was also empty, though she saw that someone had started a fire at some point. Before she left, Abigail threw a couple more logs on the fire. She didn't like being in this room alone. It always felt as though someone was watching her. Despite the heat, her skin prickled, and her mind warned her to leave.

No one was there.

The only other pair of eyes to be found were the wolf's eyes in the mural above the mantel. It was a great beast. She wouldn't have believed a werewolf existed if it weren't for the large pelt on Helicant's bed.

While the wild things on this island once existed in some form or another, the bulk of Nathaniel's diary was likely exaggerated. The werewolf, for example, was just an overgrown wolf. Abigail assumed the intention was to return home with grand tales of monsters, but for whatever reason, the family stayed.

The mural depicted the founders of the island, Nathanial and his family, hunting the werewolf down to destroy it. Its fangs barred to the full moon, and its scraggily black and gray coat painted a grisly picture. Arrows lodged in the poor beast's back as it stared in feral horror.

Enough of this place.

Trotting down the stairs, through the formal dining hall, and into the kitchen, she found Helicant asleep at the worktable. She thought about letting the old woman sleep on, but daylight was already overhead. The old woman would be livid if she woke up to discover a nap threw her off schedule.

Instead, Abigail went back into the formal dining room and searched for something to knock over. With two fingers, she gently tipped a candelabra over. It fell to the side with a clank as she walked away. It rolled off the side table and crashed even louder on the floor while Abigail made her way back up the stairs and into Destiny's bedroom to look for something more suitable to wear.

Stroking the soft lace, she marveled at the detail of the pearl buttons on her cousin's gown. Destiny would need a corset, no doubt. Abigail found the corset in the bottom of her armoire. It was a little dusty, but Abigail shook it out the best she could and laid it on the bed beside the stockings and undergarments.

She debated on whether to include the little frilly garters, but Destiny might start hyperventilating. Ribbons would suit.

Taking the dress down, Abigail pressed it against herself and looked at it in the mirror. The dress was so elegant and detailed. Her mother was a dressmaker, yet nothing she owned would ever be so fine. Doctors didn't need fancy clothing. Not for pulling calves or doling out medicine, but just once, she wanted to wear something beautiful. To be beautiful.

Vanity must've run in the family. She had to fight Joseph for the mirror on most days. Maybe that was where her resentment lay. Living in a two-bedroom house with two brothers and her parents was growing more difficult with each passing year.

Pulling the dress away, she examined the red plaid dress she was wearing. It was a little too short in the arms and too full in the skirt. She had always been tall and lanky like her father. The hand-me-downs that rotated throughout the island were never long enough.

Frowning at her dark, frizzy hair and long, thin face, she wondered if her mother didn't put as much effort into her clothes because she wasn't as beautiful as Destiny. She sighed and pushed the thoughts out of her mind. This was her younger cousin's special day. Act like it.

Voices came from outside Destiny's bedroom window. Abigail pushed the window open and called down, "What are you two do-ing?"

Destiny and Sophie shielded their eyes from the early afternoon sun. "My dress was filthy. We're going to Beth's to see if I can't borrow one from her."

"I'm afraid I have a similar problem," she said. "Mind if I borrow something of yours, Des?"

"Not at all, just as long as it's not the one hanging up."

"I found your corset, by the way."

"I hate you," Destiny said with a scowl.

"See you two soon!" Abigail said as she shut the window.

Going through her cousin's wardrobe only confirmed to Abigail that her mother did all her best work for Destiny. It was more about impressing Helicant than it was about Destiny, she knew. Coral was the sister of Destiny's father. Her mother was always nervous attending occasions at the mansion. Maybe Helicant never approved of her sister-in-law. If there was an issue, it was never known to Abigail. It was probably all in her mother's head.

Pulling out a black frock, she tilted her head in confusion. With a high lace neckline and a clingy fabric, somewhat scandalous. She had never seen Destiny wear it. It was a much more mature look than anything her cousin would wear. And it was long. Long enough to sweep against her bare ankles, like it was meant for her.

Slipping off her ragged brown dress and apron, Abigail stepped into the silky dress and fastened the buttons around the nape. She let out a gasp as she looked at herself in the mirror. Pulling back her hair, her thin, delicate neck was absolutely seductive. Borrowing some clips from Destiny's jewelry stand, Abigail was every inch a woman in her prime.

The bedroom door came open. She jumped as she came face to face with her royal crankiness herself. Abigail let out a chortle and covered her mouth. "You scared me!"

"I'm sorry, my dear, you gave me a surprise as well," Helicant said. "Where is your cousin?"

Abigail wasn't sure if she was supposed to tell Helicant or not. "They are retrieving Beth, I think."

"Oh," she said with a slight shrug. Helicant seemed to have lost interest at the mention of Beth, and her eyes fell onto the dress. "That's quite stunning on you."

Abigail blushed at the compliment.

"If I may make a suggestion..."

Before Abigail could even reply, a long, thin hand was in Destiny's jewelry chest, and she produced a long strand of pearls. Despite her diminutive size, there was always a lingering dread that one felt around the matron. A fox is small, but if it bares its teeth, you know to leave it alone—Helicant was the same way. Her eyes were focused on Abigail's neck, and she swallowed hard, though she couldn't explain why.

It was just a feeling that at any minute, Helicant's mouth would grow unnaturally wide across her face as she sprouted fangs from her gray gums and took a bite...

The rope of pearls wrapped around her neck twice. The first row lay across her chest while the second hung several inches lower. Abigail stared at herself in the mirror as she gently touched the pearls. "It's perfect."

Helicant nodded. "It may be Destiny's special day, but you'll find yourself receiving plenty of attention tonight."

Abigail let out a sarcastic laugh. "I'm afraid my options are slim."

If she didn't want to resort to incest—Abigail would rather die first. That left one man on the island for her to marry. Drew. The doctor's son. They were the same age and spent a great deal of time together when they were children, but those were not fond memories.

Helicant waved as she departed the room. "I'll be in my room dressing."

"Need me to help with anything?"

"Ready the formal dining hall."

Abigail thought about what Helicant said and what she didn't say. She adjusted the pearls one more time and fidgeted with her hair.

They weren't children anymore. Perhaps she was wrong to avoid Drew the way she did. Abigail made it a habit of steering clear of Beth, and Drew was always hunting or working the fields. He must've been healthy, as she never had to check on him. All she truly knew of Drew was the abysmal tone Edward took when he mentioned his son. It was a similar disappointment when her mother spoke of her.

Neither of them was what their parents wanted. Perhaps she and Drew had more in common than she thought.

Helicant

Helicant was sleeping in the kitchen. However, she must have been awake on some level because she was aware of the soft footsteps outside the kitchen. Someone was in the yard. It may have been just a dream, but the voices and names were too familiar to be a coincidence.

With her mind hovering somewhere between dreams and reality, Helicant's mind created its own version of events, as minds often do.

"Drew!" A man called. "Drew!" Only it wasn't a man at all. It was a great black bear standing on its hind legs. Its maw was open and gleaming with pink gums and white teeth the size of shrimp forks.

The young man snarled, ready to defend himself, but recovered when he saw just how close the great bear was. One swipe from that paw, and he'd be done for. Helicant saw the young man—who may or may not have been her nephew Drew—reaching behind his back as if he were hiding something.

"I'm here, father." He said it in a way that a perfect son should, but that couldn't be Drew.

"What are you doing clear over here?" The bear asked.

"I'm just looking at the forest," The young man said. "It's going to be fall time before we know it."

"Hm." The bear turned to the forest. It seemed to Helicant that the bear wanted to say something more but didn't know how to approach the topic. She decided that whatever dream she was having was an absurd and pointless one, but she was too tired to wake just yet.

"Well." Drew clapped his hands together. "We should go and see if the ladies need our help."

"There's something I'd like to ask you about," The bear stopped the young man. "Just between you and me."

She noted the worry creasing the black bear's brow. Just what precisely did a bear have to worry about? Had the boy taken all the fish from the stream or plucked all the berries from the bushes? Honestly, she had more important things to do than listen to this drivel, but the dream was new, and she couldn't deny the need for something fresh.

"Your mother found her distilling equipment returned to its rightful place."

Drew let out a sigh of relief. "That's good, yes?"

The bear nodded his head. "I don't blame a young man for trying his hand at moonshine now and then, but next time, let me in on it. I can better protect you from your mother."

The young man who could have been Drew laughed at the notion of distilling moonshine. It was obvious to Helicant that the young man wasn't making moonshine, but the bear was clearly approving of the idea. Of course the bear would approve, Helicant mused.

"One other thing," The bear added. "You brought home a pair of hares the other day."

"I did."

At this, the bear shifted his great weight from one back leg to the other, clearly troubled as he struggled to find the right words. "I happened upon a hare burrow. All seven kits were decapitated."

Oh, how delightful. Now this was interesting.

The young man might've been Drew had gone. Someone else had taken his place. At some point, the young man wandered too far into the forest, and something else returned, wrapped in his skin. Not that Helicant minded, just so long as he left her Destiny alone.

The young man said nothing. His arm still reached for the harness behind his back. Just what did the boy intend to do? They were near the woods. He could kill the old bear and drag his body into the forest. It would take weeks, even months, to find the bear. If they didn't find the body before fall, they may never find it. Just one slip of his blade, and none would be the wiser.

"Why did you kill the hare's offspring in such a way?" the bear asked, scratching his head with a claw.

"Better than starving or being eaten alive."

"Why take the heads?" The bear asked.

"I didn't. An animal must have gotten to them."

Helicant couldn't tell if the bear believed the man or not, but it no longer mattered. The bear was old and tired. In his uncertainty, the bear moved to all fours. He was backing down. The bear turned away and relaxed his composure. Buying the lie because it was easier. Typical.

"I didn't mention it to your mother. Next time, just stab them through the hearts or drown them."

"Yes, sir," the imposter replied.

His own father couldn't tell the real Drew from the changeling from the forest. It might've been sad had her nephew been a man of merit, but no one would ever notice he wasn't the child her sister bore.

The forest had changed him. Not for the better nor the worse, just different. It was only natural that the changeling didn't want a bear in his territory come the fall.

Helicant's eyes opened wide.

She had fallen asleep in the kitchen like some common scullery maid. Either no one knew, or everyone did. Nerves tingled with embarrassment, but perhaps no one noticed. She stretched and leaned against the back of the chair as she let out a sigh.

Turning her head to the window, she didn't so much as raise an eyebrow at the red smear of blood dripping down the cracked glass.

"And thus, it begins."

Destiny

They caught Beth just as she was coming up the lawn. Sophie waved at her twin, and Beth waved back. She was thicker around the hips, and her hair was wrapped in a tight bun. Their faces were similar and yet not. Sophie had more wrinkles around the eyes, while her sister had a myriad of creases around the lips and her jowls hung lower. They might've been identical at birth, but their personalities shaped their faces just as much as their parentage.

With one keen glance, Beth already knew that Sophie was in distress. Beth frowned and veered straight to her twin and took her hand.

Destiny had always longed for someone to know her in such a way. To understand her fears with a glance, ready to lend their strength to muddle through life together. Mothers were different in that they understood their children's potential more than they knew their actual children—at least that's the way it was with Helicant.

"My dress is all dirty," Sophie said.

Beth put an arm around her twin, and the three of them went back down the hill to the doctor's cottage. It was twice the size of Sophie's, or perhaps it was just so tidy that it felt that way. With two bedrooms, same as the cottage by the sea, it was more refined with a stone floor and plenty of rugs and drapes over the notoriously drafty windows.

The moment Destiny stepped through the door, she noted it was much warmer than even the mansion. It wasn't the heat from the fire that was supplied with a tall stack of wood by the hearth, but rather a wet warmth. Along with the humidity, she picked up the scent of new growth.

While Beth led Sophie to her bedroom, Destiny lingered around the kitchen area with its great big pot hanging over the makeshift brick oven. The backdoor was open and led into a substantial observatory that was doubling as a hot house.

The room was full of all sorts of vials and little heating cups. Dried herbs hung from the ceilings and shelves. A notebook sat on a desk with a strange bulbous pod. Raised garden beds and a well-worn copper device with long tubes that connected several fat bellies.

There was so much she didn't know, and Destiny suddenly wished to know what each and every thing in the room did. Perhaps she could become Beth's understudy and one day take the place of their only naturalist.

Along the far side of the room was a table with a white cloth. Each and every one of the doctor's implements were laid out beside his leather doctor's bag. This must've been where they cleaned his utensils. Among them were scalpels, needles, scopes, hearing devices, and a large clamp-like thing she subconsciously knew to be for childbirth.

She hoped she'd never learn the purpose of such a thing. That was enough insight into doctoring for one day.

"What I don't understand," Sophie said while stripping out of her dress. "Is how the whole cottage filled with that must dust within less than an hour."

Beth rummaged through her hope chest and withdrew a black dress like the one she was wearing. "Here we are."

"It must have been the chimney," Destiny said, leaning against the doorway. "When was the last time it's been cleaned?"

Sophie shook her head before stepping into Beth's dress. "Soot maybe, but dust? As if it settled there, and the cobwebs!"

Beth came up behind her sister and buttoned the back of the dress. "Maybe you've finally lost your marbles. Happens to the best of us, love."

Sophie rolled her eyes, but before she could reply, the buttons were fastened around her neck, and she made a choking noise that Destiny found hilarious. "This dress fits me perfect," Sophie admired in the freestanding mirror.

"It fit me perfectly ten years ago, too," Beth said.

Sophie eyed her sister up and down before saying, "What have you been doing these last ten years?"

"Eating my feelings, what does it look like?"

Destiny let out an embarrassed laugh. The sisters became so frank when they were in one another's company, she didn't know how to react.

"Marriage does that to a woman." Sophie agreed, sending a pointed glance Destiny's way.

"Shh," Beth said.

"Oh," Destiny shook her head. "It's all right."

In truth, she craved their frankness. Her father died when she was a child, and Mother cursed his memory with silence for reasons Destiny didn't understand. She had no idea what to expect when it came to marriage other than it was work. Everything on the island required hard work, but the hows remained a mystery.

Both of her aunts turned to face her then. Destiny swallowed hard as her mouth ran dry. She was so thirsty all of a sudden. It wasn't that she hadn't thought about it; in fact, it was all Destiny had thought about since her mother made the announcement. Despite all the thinking, there had been no conclusion on just how she felt.

Sophie sat beside Destiny on the quilted bed and took her hand.

"How are you feeling about this marriage?" Sophie asked.

"Daniel is my best match. I can't care for the house on my own. His family will fill the house, so I won't feel so lonely."

"But how do you feel?" Sophie pressed.

Destiny had many feelings. Those included the fear of screaming the moment her eyes met his. The shame she felt at being unable to control her worst impulses. The dread of injuring a man who she once adored as a child.

"Feel…" Among the many things Helicant told her about marriage, feelings were not one of them. "I'm frightened that I'm going to be an utter embarrassment that frightens him away, shames my mother, and convinces everyone I'm too unwell to perform the one role this island requires."

"Is that all?" Beth scoffed. "Sounds perfectly normal to me."

Destiny blinked and waited for the boot to drop, but it seemed her aunt was being serious. "Try to save the screaming for the wedding night."

Destiny's eyes went wide, and her belly went liquid. So intent on facing her green-eyed husband, she hadn't considered the wedding night itself. Somewhere in her mind, a levee broke, and even more fears came flooding out.

"Beth!" Sophie chastised.

"Oh, come on," Beth said. "You remember how our sister explained matrimonial affairs. Sat us down with a book and left it at that."

"Perhaps one worry at a time," Sophie said. "She still has to face him without... Well, I'm sorry, sweetheart, I don't entirely understand."

Beth sighed. "She has a phobia of green eyes."

"I thought you had night terrors," Sophie asked Destiny.

"The night terrors and my phobia are one and the same." Destiny sat on the bed, sinking between her aunts. "Mother insists that the dreams started after I stayed with Sophie, but they came well before that. It was only when I saw it written down in a book that I realized it was more than just a nightmare."

Sophie gasped. "I remember that. Your mother came to me furious for allowing you to read filth or some other. She was so angry that she slapped me and threatened to burn down my cottage if I ever allowed you to read another one of my books."

Beth's face scrunched. "How dare she come at you like that? After all you've done for her."

"She has a wicked temper," Sophie agreed. "But I can't leave her on her own. Go on, Destiny, tell us more."

"Well, my dream is just as Nathaniel's diary describes. I am running through Sallows Hall, lost and frightened—but I'm looking for something important. I turn down a corridor and find a long hallway with only one door at the very end, and it has one of those holes you look through..."

"A peephole?" Beth asked.

"Yeah, a peephole," Destiny agreed. "Which is weird because those belong on doors looking out, not interior doors. There are windows running along one side, but the only view through the windows is some other part of the mansion. I have no sense of direction or orientation. The other wall is plain; it's wallpapered, but no side tables or pictures."

"I go to the door at the end of the hall, and I can hear chains clinking and someone pounding and screaming from the other side. He's begging me to open the door. I'm so frightened, but I'm compelled to look."

Sophie and Beth exchanged glances, but what information they relayed was only known between them. Destiny continued to the worst part of the dream.

"The room is full of hanging chains, rusty traps on the floor. There are spikes jutting from the walls, and the floor is littered with rotting flesh and garbage. The only things living in the room are maggots and a scarred, hideous man with green eyes. He's screaming in agony and pleading for me to open the door.

'Please, Destiny, please open the door,' he says.

"I want to help him, but I can't...I just can't do it. He sees me take a step back, and he is so distraught that he rams his face into the spiked wall and takes out one of his eyes."

Neither aunt said anything for several moments. Her aunts must think the inner workings of her mind as cruel and maladapt as she.

It's Beth who speaks first. "Oh Destiny, darling, that is a terrible nightmare to have."

Destiny sniffed and wiped away the tears. "That's just it," she said, her face growing hot as her cry became a sob. "It's the only one I have."

Sophie pulled her in for a hug. "You mean you don't have other dreams? Other nightmares?"

"This is it," she said, her sarcasm slipping through the tears. "Sometimes I have nice dreams of sitting in a field of yellow flowers, but then everything melts away, and I'm in the hallway once again."

Beth shook her head. "This can't be right. Have you ever spoken to Edward about this?"

"He's tried to help me, but there's nothing he can do. My father wanted to send me to a hospital offshore, but he died before he had a chance."

"What does Helicant say?" Beth asked.

"She and I talk about it a lot. She tells me about other people who've suffered from similar ailments. She says it will take time for me to overcome mine."

"This is true," Beth agreed. "Perhaps the reason why you keep having the same dream is because it's been given so much power over the years."

Destiny agreed with that. She felt better after crying and talking about it. Once her face was dry, she straightened. "That's why I didn't outright decline the engagement. I was quite fond of Daniel as a child. If I could just grow accustomed to seeing green eyes, I could just get past my idiotic fear."

"Well, I think you'll find him to be every bit as kind as he was then. He's a gentle soul," Sophie said.

"And smart," Beth added.

Sophie gave a nod. "He's clever, for sure. He likes books. I think you'll find him open-minded and sympathetic to your problem."

She thanked them both. Destiny still couldn't free herself from the pressing anxieties that lurked in the moments of silence, but there was a lightness that came with sharing her fears. With Sophie dressed, the three women made their way back to the dark house on the hill.

Destiny squinted and used her hand to shield her eyes from the sun. Her aunts both had large, floppy hats with heavily starched flowers decorating the rims. Destiny would rather go blind than wear one of those hats. Then again, she probably wouldn't care what she wore if she went blind.

They had very little in the way of paint on the island. This was fine for the cottages as they were made of stone and mud, but the mansion was another story. It had a stone foundation, but the siding was wood.

Sophie said that the entirety of the Sallows clan came with three ships by sponsorship of the king of England. Some of the sailors stayed behind to start a new life and built a settlement the size of a small village. As their numbers dwindled, so did the resources when no other ships came to their shores.

"I don't suppose you know if your mother is handing down the ring today or not?" Sophie asked.

A cold gust from the ocean whipped over the trio just then, forcing Destiny to wrap her arms around her shoulders. "I don't know."

Beth straightened at the comment but said nothing.

"I would need to say yes first," Destiny said, though she wasn't certain that she wanted it.

"It comes with great responsibility," Beth said.

"Shh," Sophie said. "She knows that."

"To wear the ring is to be the head of the Sallows family," Beth insisted.

Destiny was listening, but she couldn't help but become distracted by the house. They were coming along the east wing, which was mostly closed. She only ever saw it from the outside. It occurred to her that there were more windows running along that wing than on the west wing.

"What is it dear?" Sophie asked.

Destiny broke her stare to look at her aunt, who was now stopped and staring at her. She looked back at the house and said, "It just seems like the east wing is much bigger than on the blueprint in your cottage."

Sophie looked at the house, her head moved from side to side as she appraised Sallows Hall. "Hm, yes, I can see what you mean. From this angle, it looks that way."

"Sallows Hall is in the shape of a capital H," Beth said without slowing.

"Well," Sophie said. "That is how it was originally mapped, but your mother wasn't the first to close off unused parts of the house."

Beth said absolutely nothing. It was as if she didn't hear a single thing. If Destiny didn't know better, she'd think Beth resented the house, or perhaps she resented who owned it.

"I'm going to see what's what in the kitchen," Sophie said with a gentle pat on Destiny's arm.

Up the stairs and behind the closed doors of the drawing room came a loud, booming voice followed by laughter. Beth shook her head and clicked her tongue. "He's had a few. Come on, let's get up there before he tells another hunting story."

"I have to get dressed."

"Oh!" Beth said. "You do, don't you? Your mother would be furious if you walked in like that. You sneak up to your room. I'll find Abigail."

Destiny was relieved with the order. She skipped up to the third floor and saw signs that Abigail had indeed already arrived and had borrowed one of her gowns. Destiny's eyes stung with sleepiness. She wasn't ready to wake this morning and longed to rest her eyes, even if only for a few moments. There was still so much that needed to happen.

Destiny had to marry, become the matriarch of Sallows Island, and overcome her worst fear all in one day. A little rest might sustain her for what came next.

CORAL

"Will you just come on!" Coral yelled at her youngest son.

When it came to Joseph, Coral wasn't above grabbing him by his ear and dragging him to the mansion if need be. It was the most important day of their lives, and her teenage son dragged his feet along the dirt path as though it were some awful choir. Gods forbid he muster an ounce of maturity for his brother's sake.

Meanwhile, the groom walked with his head down and hadn't touched his breakfast that morning. Hands in his pockets, Daniel walked to his own wedding as though it were an execution. Didn't they know this was a good thing?

"I'm coming," Joseph said. "I just don't see the point is all."

Coral turned and gave her son a most menacing glare. "You don't see the point of attending your own brother's wedding?"

Joseph knew he was walking a fine line, but he continued treading along her last nerve all the same. "She's weird. She's going to run away screaming when she sees him."

"Daniel may be a bit overweight, but hardly something to run away in fear over. Drew is another story…"

"Not because he's fat," Joseph explained. "She has these bad dreams about a monster with green eyes; she freaks out if you even mention it."

Coral knew something of it.

Helicant's mother had strange phobias that made her afraid to even leave the house. She herself had weak nerves. Just thinking about Helicant was enough to make Coral's stomach knot up. That old witch never missed anything.

Coral reached into the pocket of her apron and felt for her sewing kit. She always kept it on hand in case of emergencies.

What if Destiny tore her dress or popped a button? Coral would be ready to save the day. She had some string, several needles, a threader, a thimble, and a small pair of sharp scissors with a crane embellished on the handle. The images of her saving the day and receiving Helicant's nod of approval soothed her nerves for the time being.

Eyeing her eldest son, it made sense why he was so worried. If Destiny did indeed have some inherited malady, she may reject Daniel in front of the whole Sallows clan. Joseph may have been right. What if this whole thing was just for show, and Destiny had no intention of marrying him? Just a song and dance to pander to Coral's family before joining Edward's?

Destiny never struck her as the manipulative, calculating type. Helicant, yes, but the girl was sweet, and the intended were close as children.

"I don't imagine Destiny would agree to marriage under false pretense," Coral said, eying Daniel.

She looked to her husband for support. Perhaps he would offer advice or a gentle word, but Carl was too busy sweating. And rather profusely at that. It wasn't even midday, and his skin was gleaming from every pore. Was he ill?

He used a handkerchief to wipe his forehead, but by the time he wiped his head and neck, his forehead was already wet again.

"Are you all right, dear?" She asked.

"I'm fine; it's just the sun," Carl replied.

It was indeed warming up, and they were all dressed in black. Carl had black trousers, a black long-sleeved shirt, and a vest underneath a jacket. "Take off your jacket," she urged. "Put it back on when we arrive."

Carl nodded in agreement and did as she suggested. He gave her a faint smile and offered his arm. Coral couldn't help but be charmed by his sweet gesture.

"All you need to know about being a good husband you've already learned from your father, Daniel."

"I have to marry her first," Daniel said. "If she'll even have me."

"You just have to get to know her, is all," Carl called back to their son. "Be yourself."

"She liked me when we were children, before the nightmares," Daniel said.

Joseph cringed, and a little smile slid across Daniel's face. Coral thought the reaction from her youngest was strange but let it go.

"Maybe she'll have a new stick to beat Joseph with," Daniel said pointedly at Joseph.

Oh, she had nearly forgotten about that day! The whole family—with the exception of Joseph, burst into laughter.

"Tell us again, Daniel," she chided. Anything to distract them all from nerves.

"Well," Daniel started. "Destiny wasn't always afraid of things. She was a bit rowdy when we were children. Anyways, Drew and Joseph had me cornered along the outside of the hedge maze, and they were hitting me with switches. When out of nowhere comes little Destiny with a full branch. She spun around in circles, trying to swing it, and hit Joseph in the head."

Carl had to use the handkerchief again, this time, to wipe his eyes. Her corset nearly buckled, but the laugh was worth it.

It was meant to be a joyful day, after all.

With Daniel married to the next matron, it only made sense that the groom's family come to live in the mansion. Real wood floors. Enough room that her children wouldn't pile into one bedroom. She and Carl could sleep in a fine bed and not walk miles to work the fields and see to the animals.

Though, with Destiny marrying Daniel, there was no woman available for Joseph. The Sallows married cousins for the sake of prosperity, but to marry siblings was not right. Joseph had to realize this. Coral decided she would excuse Joseph's bad attitude tonight.

"I still have a scar from that," Joseph reminded, rubbing the spot on his forehead.

"A little scaring makes men look quite handsome, I think," Coral said.

"Indeed, battle wounds make a man," her husband agreed.

"I don't know if I would describe it as a battle," Daniel quipped. "His opponent was a five-year-old girl."

"I couldn't hit her back."

"You were nine; all you had to do was take the branch from her," Daniel argued.

Carl's face was a shade of a beet from holding in his laughter. Helicant was so angry, but she never scolded Destiny over the incident. Instead, she took it out on the good doctor. "I remember now," Coral said. "Destiny had to wear bandages for weeks after that; she tore her hands bloody holding that branch."

"It was twice her size," Joseph was still defending himself. "She could barely pick it up."

"It was quite brave of her to stand up to older boys," Carl added. "Even if her methods were a bit extreme."

"A bit? She's always been crazy."

Coral agreed with Helicant's assessment despite Destiny's aversion to green eyes. Joseph was too immature to marry, and he would never be able to provide the emotional support Destiny required. She could see Joseph marrying later in life once he had grown to love something other than his own reflection.

She worried about the future of her sons. There wasn't much in the way of opportunity on the island. Coral supposed the founders of the island didn't intend for it to be this way. There were many generations between Nathaniel's and theirs, yet the population never seemed to grow.

According to Sophie, it was nothing but rotten luck. People died in childbirth, in accidents, illness, all the normal things. But Coral couldn't help but feel there was more to it. She didn't believe the island was cursed as Helicant did, but Coral thought more about it than Beth, who didn't care at all about the past.

She had many unusual conversations with Beth while they performed the weekly laundry chore. Whenever there was mention of Sophie, the topic of history always came up.

"Sophie might be on to something," Coral once said while they washed the sheets in a rusty tin sink. "Knowing what didn't work keeps us from wasting our time."

"Mistakes are made because we lack options," Beth argued. "We're seldom given a right and wrong choice. More often, it's between bad and worse options. Go without painkillers or waste precious time and resources on growing opium? Kill a doe knowing it will make hunting harder next spring or go hungry now."

She had wanted to argue that the subject was more philosophical in nature, but Coral understood Beth's point. As residents, they didn't contribute to the major decisions, not like the matron. And ultimately, their decisions were practical in nature. She couldn't help but wonder if Beth saw everything in black and white or if she chose to because she didn't approve of her twin's scholarly efforts.

"How do you know you're going in the right direction?" Coral asked while scrubbing a dress against the accordion.

Beth paused from her pinning and looked at Coral. "Surely you know which way is up?"

"Well, yes, but what seems like the right path to up and progress may very well be the way to failure if you don't know it to be failure."

"As an individual, I have no way of providing progress on the scale you're implying," Beth said, folding a dry sheet. "I can only determine what's best for myself and my child."

Coral thought it strange that she didn't mention Edward in her statement, but it wasn't her place to pry. Abigail spent much of her time away from their humble cottage at the bottom of the island, mostly with Edward. It made people talk. In her heart, Coral didn't know if it was true or not and did not want to open that shell with Beth!

"I suppose you're right," Coral said. "But still, the past is a tool."

Beth snorted. "If it was such a great tool, Sophie would have done more with herself."

Coral did not wish to go there with Beth either.

Their conversation was steered—forcefully at times, to more mundane topics. About the hares Drew brought home from a hunt. Looking back on the conversation, Coral wondered if Beth thought Edward was truly cheating on her. Coral smiled at her Carl. He truly was her rock, even when he spoke about as much as one. He looked back at her and smiled without even knowing why.

"I love you, husband."

"And I love you," he said, squeezing her hand. "Everything will work out just fine."

Normally, her husband's words would've been reassuring, but Coral couldn't help but feel a sense of inexplicable dread. Something far beyond the common anxieties that plagued her. This was a fateful day. A day that would need to be noted in history or be doomed to repeat itself.

Helicant

Helicant ignored the clawing ache in her bones as she climbed the four flights of stairs to her bedroom. Destiny and the twins ran off who knows where, but at least Abigail was there. Her niece was setting up the dining room. As Helicant's feet found the last step, she heard a male voice and seethed.

With the cat away, the mouse would play.

Her bedroom was her sanctuary. It was where her corset could come off, and she could let her Gibson hairstyle down. Coal black hair framed white around her face; she appeared more youthful with her hair down. Despite being in her seventies, she still maintained her most attractive features.

Sitting at her vanity, Helicant began applying a series of concoctions on her face, neck, and décolleté. A serum to cleanse her skin that she wiped away with a soft cloth. Followed by a tonic to wash away any residue. Next, she applied her moisturizer from an amber-colored jar. Helicant's thin leg was exposed by the slit in her slip, but in this room, it mattered not.

Fanning herself until the moisturizer dried, Helicant inspected her face closely in the mirror and frowned at the lumps at the apex of her cheekbones.

She hissed at the abnormalities on her face, thinking them to be cystic, but cysts did not appear identically on each side of the face. The other points on her brow and the line of her nose had grown notably sharper.

Rippling from the surface, her true nature was emerging for all to see.

She sensed a pair of hungry eyes watching her. Eyeing the wolf pelt from her mirror, Helicant made a tisking noise at the creature. Naughty boy...

Heavy, clumsy footfalls sounded at her door. She didn't have enough time to pull on her robe before Edward entered her room. Of course it was him. Who else would burst into the room but the good doctor himself. Helicant wouldn't so much as look his way.

"I thought a gentleman would knock," she said.

"Helicant, I..." Edward breathed.

I what?

There was nothing left to say. Once drawn together by lust and a hateful need, their brief relationship was one of spite and pain. When there was nothing left to sate nor harm, they went their separate ways. Except for this drunken episode that happened every so often.

"The medicine," Edward asked, straightening his suit jacket as if he were reminding himself that he was the doctor and not the lover scorned. "Is it helping?"

Helicant licked her teeth from under closed lips and turned to look at him. As it just so happened, she needed a doctor. Perhaps he wasn't entirely useless.

"Have a look at these," she said, motioning to her cheek.

Without a moment's hesitation, Edward was on one bent knee beside her vanity, touching the sites with trembling hands. "Do they hurt?" He asked.

"No," she admitted. "I can't say for certain how long they've been there either."

"If I didn't know better, I would assume it was a part of your bone structure," Edward frowned while in deep thought. "But that's not possible. It's not swollen..."

Helicant realized that one of his hands was lingering on her naked knee. It trembled just as bad as the one touching her face. She wished she weren't alone in this never-ending twilight. Just a glimmer of hope would be a feast to her famine. An instant of recollection would be all she'd need, but there was no recognition in his eyes. Just glassy orbits full of lust for drink and flesh.

"Nothing about them seems familiar then."

"No, but we should keep an eye on it. I'll stop by tomorrow with equipment. We can measure them and make notes."

Helicant waved him off. "Abigail will be here tomorrow—just have her do it."

Edward was undaunted by the dismissal. He moved to leave but turned back around and said, "I am the doctor, not her."

"And since you have no idea what these are, it doesn't matter. Might as well pass the case on to someone who is up to the job."

Edward shook his head and growled. "I've always been up to the job.

Ah, there it was. They were no longer talking about the ridges on her face. Helicant let the last few words dangle in the air as Edward's face turned red. Here he was trying to be that good doctor, but he always failed to keep it strictly professional.

"I just think this is something I should be involved with."

If she wanted more involvement from him, Helicant would have married him instead of William. Yet, here she was, happily widowed.

"I need to get ready for the party," she reminded him. "Whiskey is in the drawing room on the mantel. You'll need some to stop that dreadful shaking."

The door slammed shut, but she was too busy preparing the next stage of her beauty regimen to care.

Opening a drawer of her vanity, Helicant produced a small paintbrush with a round knob handle. Pulling the crimson jar out of a different drawer, she dipped the brush into the red liquid and applied it to her face, neck, and chest.

The blood itched as it dried on her skin. The metallic smell filled the air, and Helicant's head rolled back as she took the time to enjoy the treatment. It was experimental. Something she had found in one of Sophie's occult books, but Helicant grew quite fond of it over the years.

She made a fresh batch recently from the blood drained from a burrow of hares. Drew never asked questions when she asked for such things. It certainly wasn't the strangest request Helicant had made of him. All the more reason she would never allow him to marry her Destiny. Hers was a practical need, but Drew was all too eager to shed blood.

A few drops of the blood rolled over her upper lip, and she unconsciously lapped it up, savoring the taste.

With a fresh, clean face, Helicant used her powder and restored her hairstyle. She washed before dressing in new undergarments. Her corset required some loosening as of late. This should have made her happy, but if she gained too much weight, she'd need a new wardrobe.

In the mirror, Helicant observed the way her breasts appeared fuller, her neck a little less creased. She gave several poses before suddenly feeling rather stupid.

"Oh, for heaven's sake," she cried out loud.

She was an old widow, not some dame who stared at herself in the mirror all day. It was Edward's visit that had her feeling this way.

Helicant entered the formal dining room on the first floor. The hand-carved table was freshly polished, and three floral arrangements now sat at three different points. The plates and silverware were placed neatly on ivory linen napkins, and even the cushions had matching new covers. Abigail walked in wearing an apron over that slinky dress, and Drew was tailing right behind her.

"Afternoon, Helicant." Abigail greeted.

Still holding the placemats, Helicant noted they were embroidered with little foxes. It must've taken months to hand-stitch them. "Did your mother do these?"

"Yeah! I brought them ahead with me. She was still fitting Daniel's suit when I left."

"You'll have to give her my regards," she said. "These are lovely, precisely what we needed."

Abigail gave a pursed smile as Drew fumbled behind her. Helicant could tell the two were getting along by the way he trailed her. "If you have everything in hand, I shall see to the drawing room and greet guests."

Her niece's cheeks flushed, and she gave a nod. Despite the slight variations, the night was going according to plan. While Drew had his hands full of Abigail, he'd have less time to sabotage Destiny's wedding.

The knock on the door echoed in the entryway. Helicant opened the door to find the groom and his vain little brother. Coral's smile was frozen on her face while she blatantly fiddled with something in her pocket, and her husband, Carl, was sweating profusely.

They were an odd couple, but she'd endure it for her daughter's sake.

Daniel stepped forward on his own and bowed. A little more formal than required, but at least he was respectful. "Hello, Mrs. Sallows. Thank you for inviting us."

Of course she would invite him; he was the groom, after all.

Biting back the response, she managed to say, "Please, come in."

Helicant played the good host; even though everyone knew where to hang up their coats, she helped them all the same. Carl's shirt clung to him and was nearly transparent with sweat. She could see his nipples. At least he didn't smell yet.

Joseph attempted to wander into the kitchen. Stepping between the boy and his avenue to mischief, she said, "Why don't you show your father to the drawing room?"

The boy managed not to roll his eyes, but he hesitated.

"Joseph, do as you're told." His mother hissed.

It was Carl who led Joseph up the stairs to the second story, leaving Helicant to walk with Coral. "I wanted to thank you for all your hard work. The placemats, cushions, and Destiny's dress."

Coral was so pleased by Helicant's praise, she looked as though she would burst through her corsets. She was a thick woman, much like William. Sometimes it pained her to see a face so familiar to her late husband, but she barely recalled his face these days.

In the drawing room, Helicant found Edward three whiskies deep into the decanter. At least he was behaving himself. He greeted everyone jovially, and while their necks steered their faces away from his stinking breath, there were smiles around the room. Even Joseph found his interest peaked by the charismatic doctor.

No one noticed when Helicant closed the pocket doors and descended the stairs. This made her smile. A good hostess helped people fit in but didn't claim all the attention. She moved through the hall towards the kitchen but heard Abigail giggle and decided to leave another way.

Everything was going splendidly.

Taking the corridor alongside the kitchen, she stiffened as she passed the room she had successfully avoided for years.

It was a passageway meant for laundry maids, really. They could come in and out through the back door and into the laundry room the way the servants would use the back door to the kitchen if they had them. Since there were scarcely enough people on this island to operate the laundry room, Coral and Beth washed clothes by hand.

Helicant's hand clasped on the brass doorknob, and she hesitated. She shouldn't go in there. It held nothing there but awful memories, but she was always drawn to the horrific. The macabre scene still burned in her mind, and Helicant needed to see the room vacant.

The door swung open, and all at once, she was lost in a fog of steam. It billowed past her and down the hallway. Smells of cleaning agents and lye filled her nostrils and stung her eyes. Helicant heard the groan of the wooden cogs that worked the old laundry machine dealing with the linens.

Who started the machines and why? The younger people of the island didn't even know how it worked. Joseph or Drew, perhaps both, must've been behind it. "Who's there?" Helicant demanded.

There was no answer. Moving through the steam—carefully so as not to fall into one of the lye troughs. She knew what happened to people who met that fate.

As if the room knew Helicant's mind, the steam lessened enough for Helicant to see a woman sitting up in one of the trenches. She had fallen face-first into the lye solution. Her skin was red and blistering, and her black hair was falling out in bloody chunks, revealing patches of bone beneath the scalp.

The woman's white dress clung to her, wet with the solution, and Helicant flinched backward. In agony and terror, the woman tried to tear the dress off, but her fingernails snapped off at the cuticles. Like most of their gowns, her buttons went up the back and couldn't be removed alone.

"Mother," Helicant whispered.

Helicant knew better now. There was no saving her mother. Even if she managed to pull her out, the lye would eat away at her skin for days and weeks. No amount of morphine would help; there was nothing she or anyone else could do.

The excruciated wail of incoherent pleading was too much even for the hell-hardened woman Helicant was today.

She understood now that her mother's spirit was not in the bed where she died by Edward's hand. Her mother's ghost remained here, not where Helicant dragged her lye-scalded body from the trough and through the corridor as she pleaded for help in the empty house.

Her hand found the wooden paddle. She should've done this years ago, but she was young and was in denial. The girl needed a way to save her mother, but the old crone understood the truth of it.

The woman's eyes were gone. Melted into the back of her mother's skull, leaving gelatin tears from black orb sockets. Some part of Helicant felt she should endure the ghastly vision as if it were yet another punishment for her existence.

She didn't ask to be made, nor did she make a pact with a devil, but sometimes Helicant wondered if they weren't right about her.

Without a second thought, she bludgeoned the image of her mother to death with the paddle. It did not wisp away as most assume spirits would; rather, the neck snapped, and the head cracked like a hard-boiled egg. Helicant's swings with the paddle were met with resistance, and with each strike, she fought to catch her breath.

When the lump of blistering flesh stopped screaming, Helicant knew her mother was truly dead after all these years. The body slumped into the lye—now tinted pink from blood. The steam evaporated, leaving Helicant with the smell of soap and iron. Dropping the paddle, she gave one final look before shutting the door and found the room to be quite empty.

There was no trace of her mother's body, of any operation whatsoever. The laundry room was an empty, dusty room like so many in Sallows Hall. How long had her mother's spirit been waiting for her? She should have known better than to think Edward had done anything right, even killing a helpless burn victim.

She didn't get so much as halfway to the kitchen before Edward's laugh rattled the walls upstairs. From one nightmare to the next, this day would be relentless.

Helicant couldn't ignore that Edward was drunk. Halfway through the whiskey decanter left on the handsome mantle, she could only watch the good doctor in sheer amazement as he retold the same old stories. No one apart from her saw him for what he was but his son.

Drew stood by the door as if he were waiting for something real to happen. Perhaps they were more alike than Helicant thought.

"...And that was how I caught the terror of the eastern wood," Edward finished.

Everyone applauded, Drew joined in but clapped silently. Helicant gave no such approval. She only glared at the village drunk. Drew continued to look at the door as if he were waiting for someone. Perhaps he and Abigail had reconnected, and he was waiting for her.

Normally, Helicant wasn't one for gossip, but she had an interest in seeing Abigail connect with someone other than that slanderous beast she had understudied.

Helicant approached the young man and whispered, "You seem to be waiting for something."

Drew laughed self-deprecatingly. "It's that obvious."

Helicant said nothing but she gave a slight grin. "I was young once."

Drew looked around the room as if he were embarrassed—they both knew better than that. "Abigail and I..."

She knew it. Helicant patted Drew on the arm and said, "I'm happy for you."

"Something about the way she looks tonight. I think this is the first time she's given me the time of day."

"I suspect the two of you will have time to reacquaint more this evening. But in the meantime, don't hover next to the door."

"Too desperate?"

Helicant enjoyed his charm. Neither Joseph nor Daniel had this ability to portray something other than what they were. Drew took after his father in that way.

Eventually, Drew joined Joseph for several minutes. He practically bore down on the younger man. Whatever Drew pressed him with, Joseph relented, and there was an exchange she couldn't interpret. Abigail hadn't proved enough of a distraction. Whatever they got up to, it wouldn't bode well.

Drew's eyes scouted the room, and Helicant was forced to look down. Joseph and Drew parted ways, and Drew began preparing cups of punch.

"And what of our bride-to-be?" Drew asked.

"She is dressing, presumably," Helicant explained. "This evening, after dinner, Daniel will propose with this." She extended a frail hand, exposing a great ruby ring set in gold.

Removing it, Helicant strode towards Daniel. She took his hand and placed the ring in his. She noted the downcast eyes and the perpetually flushed cheeks. Was he the right match for Destiny? None would know until the girl said yes.

"This is for you to give to her," Helicant told Daniel.

"A toast!" Joseph announced. "To the groom-to-be!"

Everyone made their way to the punch bowl where Drew awaited, serving everyone a glass. All save Edward, who snatched the decanter from the mantle and took a direct swig from the bottle itself. Helicant felt her face grow hot at the scene. What an embarrassment.

After several moments, everyone had crystal cups and toasted the groom. Daniel took a sip out of politeness, but he seemed none too keen on the sweetly sour taste. Helicant wasn't fond of it either. She drank the entire glass, her jawbone pinched from the sweetness.

The doors slid across their tracks, and Drew looked up hopefully to see Abigail's face. In a most comical way, that image was marred by the squat, plump woman with an oversized hat. Beth entered the room and was scowling at Edward almost as hard as Helicant was.

Beth strode up to her husband, and there was some muttering between them while everyone else pretended not to notice. Helicant rather enjoyed watching her sister ream the man for his behavior. She wasn't about to miss this for the world.

The muttering between Beth and Edward grew louder. With Edward emboldened by the whiskey and Beth's pride on the line, neither was willing to back down. "Haven't you had enough, dear husband?"

While the argument between the couple worsened, everyone was so intent on listening that no one took note of a second exchange between Daniel and Joseph. The two boys were once again conspiring in the corner.

"I don't think I have," Edward said. "Perhaps you'd like some, might make you a bit more jovial."

Coral's face went flush with the looming conflict. "Why don't we see how dinner is progressing?"

"Yes, that would be quite good," Edward said dismissively.

Drew's mother was not willing to back down. "We've talked about this. It's why I no longer distill liquor. You can't seem to put it down..."

Helicant felt her interest in the disagreement drain. She felt lithe and content with any outcome on any plane of existence, and that wasn't like her. Carl understood where she was coming from. He, too, despite his perspiration, slacked in William's favorite chair. Coral stared at her husband and even nudged him to do something about the squabble.

Carl's long fingers intertwined on his lap as he stared at the ceiling. With no support from her husband, Coral took it upon herself to intercede.

"Oh, I don't think he's hurting anyone," Coral soothed. "Come along, Beth. Let's see if Sophie needs help."

"Enough for everyone to have a good evening," Helicant overheard Joseph say to Drew.

The boys must've spiked the punch, but she couldn't muster an ounce of annoyance. Still, this night was for Destiny, and the future of their clan was at stake. Forcing herself to her feet, Helicant silenced the argument.

"Beth is right; you've had more than enough, Edward," she said, snatching the decanter from his hand. She was a foot shorter than Edward, but he had his tail between his legs when she snapped. The ring might be in Daniel's possession, but Edward knew better than to defy her.

"Beth, your sister does indeed need your help. I expect dinner to begin promptly at four."

Without another word—which was rare for her sister—Beth left the drawing room. Carl wiped a tablespoon of sweat from his forehead before joining Daniel in a game of chess. Helicant turned and observed the panic return to Daniel's face as he once again remembered he was to be the center of attention for the evening.

"Good thing you came in when you did. I was worried it would come to blows," Coral said to her.

The woman had no idea how right she was. Unfortunately for Coral, Helicant was distracted by the shenanigans around her. Everyone had a motive in this room. None of it involved Destiny's safety and well-being. They were like loose ribbons floating around the room, and Helicant was trying to determine which one was the most pressing.

That was when Drew approached his father, who was licking his wounds in the corner of the room. Helicant desperately wanted to hear what they were saying, but she would need to rid herself of Coral first.

She smiled politely and nodded. "Married couples all have their rough patches."

Coral didn't seem to know what to say to that. It occurred to Helicant that Coral and Carl never had a rough patch. How wonderful it must have been to be so blissful. The woman still wouldn't leave her be.

"I've heard about your new hobby, taxidermy?" Helicant asked.

Coral went flush as if it were something she'd rather not discuss. "I'm told it's not the most lady-like of hobbies."

"Oh, I disagree," Helicant said. "It's a beautiful hobby. One of preservation and creativity."

While Coral babbled, Helicant observed a sort of confrontation between father and son. Edward's face was red with alcohol and anger. He poked Drew with a pointed finger in the chest as if threatening him. Drew gave a vicious smile. She didn't like it.

All of a sudden, Helicant felt a wave of revolution wash over her, but why? Something in their conversation. It was a woman's intuition. Knowing an ex-lover's face and a dream that left lingering questions.

Whatever they were discussing had a profound impact on what she loved most.

"Are you all right?" Coral asked.

"Yes, I'm fine, just tired. Please, go on."

She kept a watchful eye on father and son as they parted ways. Should anything bad happen to Destiny, she would murder them both.

Sophie

Sophie hated being alone with her twin. It was like seeing what would've become of her had she had she married Edward. Bristling at the notion, she busied herself with preparing the food while Beth carried on and on—Good Gods, did the woman need breath? Sophie focused her annoyance by mashing the potatoes.

"...But I told him, I won't darn socks that have already been darned. He's just too shy to ask Coral. I told him I would go and ask her, it's not a problem."

Beth was at the stovetop, poking at the carrots and radishes in a cast iron skillet with a long fork. Could she hear herself, or had her ears ceased to work? She and her sister were always different people, but when did she become this person? So engrossed with the mundane and the petty, Beth was relentless.

"Oh, speaking of Coral." Beth paused, signifying she was about to gossip. "Did you hear about her new hobby, shall we say?"

Sophie could only stare at her sister blankly while her onions sizzled. She shook her head and began to protest, but Beth went right over the top of her.

"I stopped by their cottage, and Carl, the sweetheart, told me that Coral was in their workshop. I went up the hill and took a peek in the window. Sophie, you wouldn't believe what I saw."

"A hobbyist?" Sophie asked dryly.

The lack of interest was lost on Beth. It occurred to Sophie that Beth didn't care if she was interested or not. It didn't matter whether she was her sister or the person on the other side of the island. Technically, Sophie was both, but still. Beth made no distinction because she didn't care. Her sister was going to gossip whether Sophie wanted it or not.

"She is making taxidermy!" Beth gasped. "Not just an antler mount or a wolf pelt. She's creating her own creatures. Sitting on the table was a rabbit with antlers! Can you believe the macabre of it?"

Sophie couldn't fathom the horror. A stuffed bunny with horns. She shook her head and resumed thrashing the potatoes while Beth went on and on about the rabbit and about how it was an abomination.

When they were kids, their mother used to say they were total opposites. Sophie never thought it would divide them as adults, but somewhere along the way, Beth became someone Sophie couldn't stand. Mash, mash, mash... To her horror, Sophie was envisioning Beth's head in the bowl and smashed it down with the mallet.

"Sophie, you're getting potatoes everywhere."

"Will you just be quiet?" Sophie couldn't take it anymore. It felt like her brain would shrink away like salt on a slug.

Beth stopped prodding the vegetables. Her twin didn't look upset or even surprised by the outburst. "You're starting to sound like Helicant."

It might've been a slight on an ordinary day, but she was beyond aggravation at this point. Her sister always knew how to provoke her, but Sophie could play that game, too. "More like your husband."

Beth's plump cheeks turned a bright shade of red. Sophie enjoyed the first silent moment in the kitchen since her sister first entered. Sophie didn't turn to look and see just what her sister was doing. She had her own things to work on.

At some point, Beth stepped out, and the room became blissfully silent. She turned back to the stovetop and nearly jumped out of her skin. Helicant was standing right there.

"Goodness, Helicant. You scared me half to death."

Her older sister gave her a wry smile. "We're close to the end, sister."

"The end of what?" Sophie asked.

Helicant's smile grew and exposed a pair of sharpened canines. The lashes around the matron's eyes appeared fuller, and there was a sharpness to her features that was quite off-putting. "Are you feeling all right? You seem strange."

Her sister took a step forward, and Sophie, on instinct, stepped back. She couldn't shake the feeling that she was being stalked, but that was ridiculous. This was the woman who raised them after Mother died.

When Sophie was a child, she was afraid of monsters. Not because they lived on an island rumored to be infested with creatures—hers were the typical fears a child had alone in her bed at night.

"I'm rather fond of monsters," a teenage Helicant said from beneath her flowing black hair. "They're delicious."

Sophie believed it then, and a part of her always would. But something was off. The way Helicant spoke made her shiver. She often said odd things like that, as though the matron knew something the rest of them didn't.

"I'm fine," Helicant said. Grasping the skillet with her bare hand, she removed it from the heat.

Sophie sucked in a fresh breath of air. Destiny needed to become the matron, and soon. Her sister's mind was clearly going.

Helicant gave a quick inspection of the kitchen before asking about Beth. "Where is she?"

Sophie ducked her head down and tried to give nothing away. "I'm not sure. She stepped out for a minute."

"The two of you fighting?"

How could she know? Sophie looked to Helicant, who gave a knowing nod. "Beth is only quiet when she's angry."

"She just goes on and on," Sophie confessed. "When did she get like that?"

Helicant's footsteps were quiet as she walked around the kitchen. "You are to blame as much as she. You've become far too accustomed to living in silence, but unlike you, she is truly alone. Her husband and son despise her, as do her sisters. She has no one."

Something fell to the floor, and both women turned to find Beth standing in the kitchen doorway. Her mouth was open, but no words came out. On the floor was a basket of freshly picked eggs. Sophie's heart broke for her twin at that moment.

"Oh, Beth." She reached for her, but Beth quickly ran out the door.

"Let her go," Helicant said. "Dinner will not cook itself. I've had enough of her dramatics for one evening."

"Did you know she was there?" Sophie asked.

Helicant didn't answer. Instead, she nodded to the dumbbell waiter. "Make sure to clean that thing before putting any food in it. Perhaps you don't mind the dust in the kitchen, but I'd rather not have it in our food."

"I cleaned every countertop and the dishes before I started—" Sophie started to argue, but when she looked around, she noticed that Helicant was right. There was dust everywhere. Bits of mashed potato that flew from the bowl had a gray film over the top. The dishes were unwashed. Everything was filthy.

Much like how it suddenly overwhelmed her cottage, the dust had eroded over all the counters and unused dishware. Besides, there was no point in arguing. Helicant had already left the room.

The dumbbell waiter door was the same whitewashed color as the rest of the kitchen, with a bit of molding around it to distinguish it from the rest of the wall. It made a dry rasp as she pushed the sliding wooden door up to expose the food cart.

To her surprise, there was hardly any dust at all. Not even a spiderweb. It smelled of pine wood and oil as if it were new.

It still didn't change how Sophie felt about the device. It reminded her of the feeling she experienced when walking down basement steps. Like something was about to grab her and pull her in as the door came slammed shut. This door was too rigid in its track to simply fall; she supposed that was the intention.

All the same, Sophie left the door open to air it out.

Between the casserole baking and pie-making, Sophie took the extra time to reclean the kitchen. Helicant's words stung harder than her sister likely intended. She couldn't have known about the state Sophie's cottage was in. Still, Sophie couldn't help but feel like a lazy old slob. Taking greater care this time, Sophie made sure no counter went unattended.

When she was finished, she examined the dirt and dust on the dishcloth with disgust. How could this happen in just a few hours? Her cottage endured the same mystery. Sophie thought about a book she read where towns were covered in ash due to a nearby island's volcanic activity. She wondered if the dust was blown onto the island from another country.

While she pulled out the casserole, she dreamed of setting sail to a new world. One that was more like the books she read late at night by the fire. While she worked the dough of the pie, Sophie's bones began to ache. This happened when the weather changed or when it was about to rain. It was a dull ache that reverberated throughout her entire body. Sometimes, it started in a finger or her forearm, and the pain would wrack its way through her as if she were a gong hit by a mallet.

This time, the pain had started in her thigh. Sophie stopped what she was doing and braced herself against the counter. She sucked in deep breaths and held them for several moments. Edward had taught her this breathing method when she finally broke down and visited him last spring.

"It's actually for childbirth, but if this breathing technique helps with the pain of that, surely it can help with this," he said.

Sophie sat on the worktable Edward used to examine people in the back of his cottage. Her feet dangled as she struggled to relay her fears. "It's been happening more frequently of late."

"You're not a young lady anymore, Sophie." Edward teased.

While she appreciated his humor, she was still frightened by the pain.

"It's more than that. It's a debilitating pain that makes me shiver all over, only to end suddenly. I...I'm afraid of it."

Edward straightened, and his eyes narrowed. "I have rudimentary tools at best," he said. "But if you'll allow me, I'd like to do some bloodwork."

Sophie gave a nod of consent, and Edward brought out a small case with needles. He pulled out a strip of fabric and used it to tie off her arm before pushing the needle into her vein. The pinching sting of the needle made Sophie bite her lip. Suddenly aware of Edward's gaze, she felt flush.

Her eyes skipped from the crimson liquid filling the glass tube to the intense brown eyes staring her down. She could feel his body heat they were so close.

She felt the drawing ache as the needle was withdrawn from her arm. The tourniquet was released, but Edward remained by her side. He put a hand on her shoulders. One moment, it was comforting, and the next, he pulled Sophie into a kiss.

His beard bristled against her delicate skin, and she could smell his minty aftershave, which couldn't contain the lingering whiskey on his lips.

Sophie pushed back, forcing them apart. Edward bowed his head in shame, but she wasn't certain it was genuine. This was a situation that seemed all too practiced. Sophie wondered who else he played this scene with.

"You're married to my sister."

"I made a mistake in marrying her," he snarled. "It should have been you."

Edward went in again, nuzzling his face against hers. Temptation flared in a body long denied such affections. She was a lonely woman, and sometimes, in that loneliness, she would have bouts of crazed, desperate insanity. She could empathize with Edward because he no doubt experienced this as well, but at the moment, Sophie thankfully had her wits about her, and she saw him for what he was.

"You're a lonely beast, Edward," she said. "There's only one woman you've truly ever wanted, and we both know she isn't me."

This was enough to snap Edward into his senses. He pulled away and took up a more professional pose before taking the blood sample to his desk. "I'll see what I can with this sample. If this goes on, you may need to consider taking something for the pain."

Sophie hopped down from the table and left. She never asked for morphine. The pain that had doubled over had subsided enough that Sophie straightened and resumed rolling out the pie dough.

Her knees trembled slightly, but she otherwise felt fine.

If anything, Sophie felt a sense of exhilaration she couldn't quite describe. Euphoric.

Destiny

Destiny told herself she would try on the dress when she reached her bedroom. Passing the party in the drawing room, she knew her time was running short. Her mother would want her to be wearing the dress Coral painstakingly made. Daniel would propose, and the pact would be made.

Everyone expected something of her.

Some wanted her to fail. To take one glimpse at Daniel's eyes and faint from terror. Others, like Abigail and her mother, wanted her to say yes.

She didn't want to let anyone down, especially not her mother, but she also didn't know if she could do this thing. The very idea of being in the same room with him sent tremors through her bones. If she tried to hold back the tears, the convulsions would start, and it was like her throat was closing in on itself.

Maybe seeing a person with green eyes wouldn't have the same effect as the night terrors, but even just thinking about it was enough to send her into a panic that wouldn't end until she created a new doll to hang on a doorknob.

Even a house like this would run out of doorknobs eventually.

Taking a deep breath, Destiny shut her bedroom door and stared down the long black gown. It was beautiful. Lacy in the right places and sheer in others. It was traditional and high collar like her mother requested, but it had a sort of roguish modern style that Destiny thought was so couture.

Digging through her closet, Destiny found the corset she'd undoubtedly need to wear. She wondered if she'd still fit it. Then again, Destiny supposed it didn't matter if it fit or not. The whole point of a corset was to squeeze you until you couldn't breathe.

"Rawr!"

Destiny's heart seized in her throat, and she let out a cry of fear as she swatted harmlessly at her cousin, Abigail.

"Shit, you scared me half to death!" Destiny cried.

Abigail was laughing so hard she was snorting. Her cousin fell to the bed in a fit of hysterics, but Destiny only wanted to stop the pounding in her throat. "I can't get my heart to stop pounding. You're such an asshole."

"I'm sorry you didn't hear me come in," Abigail laughed. "I couldn't resist."

"I need your help anyways," Destiny said, holding up the corset.

"That's why I came up here."

Destiny couldn't help but notice how nice Abigail looked. She was wearing a sexy black gown without sleeves. It wasn't something she'd normally wear. Her hair was pulled back, and she looked so sophisticated. "You look beautiful."

"I should hope so," Abigail said. "It came from your closet."

Destiny shook her head. Her cousin was a foot taller than her. There was no way that dress belonged to her. "That isn't mine."

Abigail shrugged and stood, "Well, I found it in your closet. A mystery for another day. Come on, let's get that thing on."

The corset caged around Destiny's middle. The laces were tightened a little at a time, allowing her to get accustomed to them. In the meantime, she and her cousin caught up on the latest gossip. "My mother must be so annoyed right now," Destiny said while walking around her room, getting a feel for the corset.

Abigail sat on the bed and bounced a little. With her shoes off, her cousin flexed her feet. "She's on her best behavior. My mother and Edward, on the other hand…"

Destiny turned to look at her cousin for an explanation. Abigail leaned her head from side to side before confessing. "My mother is always nervous around yours, and Edward isn't much better."

"Is he drunk already?"

Abigail snickered. "Snockered."

Destiny rolled her eyes, "If it bothered Mother so much, you'd think she'd just hide the whiskey. She never does. I think she secretly likes it."

"She likes riling him up, that's for sure." Abigail agreed.

Destiny wondered why. "I know Edward courted my mother before she married my father. It seems they still have some unresolved feelings."

Abigail became unusually quiet for a moment before saying, "Time to tighten it again."

Destiny let out a frustrated groan, "Why does this all matter?"

Abigail slipped behind her, and Destiny felt the tugs against her corset once more. "One day, you're going to be old and fat like our aunts, and you're going to look back at this moment. Don't you want to feel the most beautiful?"

A sense of foreboding came over Destiny just then. It hung over her like a thick wool blanket, and she wished for once that someone could feel it, too. Sometimes, it seemed as though her mother could, but if she did, Helicant was not the sort of woman to give up her secrets.

"What if I freak out?" Destiny breathed against the corset. She could feel her ribs bend to the garment's will.

"Just give him a chance," Abigail implored. "Give yourself a chance."

Destiny had avoided Daniel for all these years. She felt terrible about it. He was a sweet boy when they were kids. He didn't deserve to be treated like the monster from her nightmares. It wasn't his fault he had green eyes, but just thinking about those eyes made the wool blanket all the more stifling.

Destiny inhaled again and again, but there was no satisfaction to be had. She couldn't breathe in this thing. "I can't do this," she said.

Abigail took her hands and led her to the bed. "Just rest a while. Get accustomed to that corset. You want something to drink from downstairs?"

Laying on the bed did help, Destiny admitted. "No, I'm fine. I just need to get this over with."

It was just Daniel. The bookish boy who once showed her an encyclopedia of the island's bugs. Everyone loved him, so maybe she could too. It wasn't like she had any other option. Joseph was... Well, Joseph. And there was something about Drew that made her skin crawl. He came by the house often, but Destiny didn't know why. He would knock on the back door, and her mother would greet him and take him down to the basement.

"I saw Drew here again," she asked one night over dinner. "What does he come here for?"

Her mother didn't so much as look up from her plate. "He brings dinner, of course."

Destiny was sheltered, not an idiot. "So late at night?"

Helicant's knife sawed at the meat on her plate. "Sometimes he doesn't get back from a hunt until late."

"But we get meat once it's cleaned and skinned from their house..."

The knife scraped against the porcelain plate, and Helicant finally looked up at her. "We are right next to the forest. He can bring me much fresher meat if I just clean it myself instead of waiting for Beth to get around to it."

"Sorry," Destiny whispered.

Helicant sighed and set her utensils down. "No, it is me who should be sorry. You're just asking why a man is at our door in the dead of night. I'm tired, is all. My sleep was disturbed."

Her mother slept on the fourth floor. There was no way she could hear Drew knocking at the kitchen door from her room. Her mother was expecting and waiting for him. She just didn't know why it was such a secret.

Destiny shifted on the bed to get more comfortable. As long as she didn't excite herself too much, the corset was bearable. Once she got up, she'd no doubt be unable to breathe again. Abigail was humming sweetly while she touched up her hair in the mirror. She was like a masterpiece depicted in the books about Europe.

"I didn't realize how similar you and Joseph look until now," Destiny told her.

"Everyone talks about how handsome he is but never mentions my looks."

"That's because all Joseph has is a pretty face."

Abigail grimaced. "I know, the poor boy. You know we've all tried. Daniel is the only one who hasn't given up on him. He spends hours and hours working with Joseph on how to read and never once gets angry with him."

"He doesn't know how to read?"

Abigail paused and looked at her through the mirror. "You're not supposed to know that."

"It's just so sad. I'd be so lonely if I couldn't read."

"He's getting better," Abigail said. "He'll never be able to read anything substantial, but he can read basic things now."

Destiny stared at the tiles on the ceiling. "That's really nice of Daniel to teach him."

"Daniel says it's not his fault. Something about the letters appearing out of order."

"Like a disorder?" She couldn't help but relate. If Daniel was patient enough to teach Joseph to read, he might just be patient enough to deal with her condition.

"Yeah, he called it something..." Abigail was too engaged with her hair to recall.

What if all she needed to get better was to work with someone kind and understanding like Daniel. He knew how caterpillars turned into butterflies and why the waves came and went from the shore. Destiny would've never guessed that the moon was involved.

"We all hide our shortcomings."

There was a knock at the door. Destiny couldn't sit up. She merely turned her head towards the door as Abigail opened it just a crack before letting Coral into the room.

"Uh," she said with a mixture of humor and alarm, "Can someone help me?"

Coral and Abigail both giggled at her plight, but they each extended a hand to pull her upright. Her vision speckled as the world swayed. "Phew."

"I just wanted to make sure the dress fit okay," Coral said. "My dear, you're not even dressed yet."

She had delayed as long as she could. Coral and Abigail pulled the dress over her raised arms. The material slipped over her corset and underclothes with just enough slack that the buttons created a snug fit. Deft fingers worked up the back while Abigail used the lacing tool to button her boots.

"Can't I just wear my shoes?" Destiny pleaded. "Mother won't notice."

Abigail shot her a look, and Destiny relented. "Okay, she would notice, but she would forget about it.

Coral eyed her daughter up and down with a disapproving expression. "Where did you get that dress anyhow?"

Destiny and Abigail both paused and gave Coral a confused look. She was the only seamstress on the island. Who else would make it but her?

"I borrowed it from Destiny's closet."

"It suits you quite nice, like it was tailored for you!"

Abigail promptly stood up and stomped out of the room. "If only I had someone to tailor such finery for me!"

Destiny felt for her cousin. Coral didn't approve of Abigail becoming a doctor for some reason. Coral had finished buttoning her dress and was checking the fit over the rest of the dress as if her daughter had not just run out of the room.

"It fits perfectly," Coral said.

"Thank you," Destiny didn't know what to say without making things more awkward. She wanted to defend Abigail, ask Coral why she gave Abigail the leftover or discarded gowns. Why didn't she appreciate how clever her daughter was?

Destiny wasn't a doctor. She couldn't sew, she certainly wasn't a hunter or botanist. If it were not for her mother, Destiny would have nothing to offer. She was not in a position to question the people she relied on the most. This woman was soon to be her mother-in-law.

"Anything else you need, dear?" She asked.

It wasn't words that came to Destiny's mind, but rather an overall feeling she wanted to convey. It wasn't right the way Coral dismissed Abigail, and while she didn't think it right to call it out directly, Destiny wanted her to know where she stood.

"You can go and retrieve Abigail for me," Destiny said in her best Helicant voice. "I need her."

Coral blinked. It was as if she forgot her daughter was even in the room. Perhaps Destiny misinterpreted the expression on the woman's face because she shook her head as if she didn't understand the request. "It would be wise to keep her at a distance."

"Why?"

Coral turned away. "You're to be a married woman soon. Abigail walks a different path."

Destiny's face scrunched. What a load of dung. "What does that even mean?"

"I don't think she cares all that much about marriage vows. Abigail is a selfish girl. She takes what she wants."

Before she could question Coral further, the woman walked out of the room, leaving Destiny alone. What could she possibly be going on about? Destiny let out a noise in disgust and tried to let the comments go by looking in the mirror at her dress.

She didn't want to admit it, but Destiny couldn't remember a time when she felt more beautiful.

Her hair still laid limply, and her eyes still had that haunted look, but the black was a stark contrast against her pale skin. The corset made her look as though she were molded into the dress, giving a sculpted look. She looked regal... She looked like her mother.

A timid knock at the door sounded Abigail's return. She was winded as if she ran back up the stairs, but otherwise, she seemed okay.

"I need help with my hair."

HELICANT

Helicant turned and found herself face to face with Coral. The woman's eyes glistened with tears as if she were about to cry, but her lips were upturned in a shaky smile. It occurred to her that Coral had been talking to her for some time and that she wasn't listening.

"What is it, my dear?"

"The dress," Coral said. "Has she tried it on?"

She noted Coral fidgeting with something in her apron pocket. She had overlooked her sister-in-law once again. It wasn't that she disliked the woman; on the contrary, any feelings she had were neutral. Nothing had changed Helicant's impression of the woman since the day Coral was brought into the world all red-cheeked and squalling.

"I don't know, but if there is a problem, I'll be sure to let you know."

This did not seem to placate the nervous woman before her. If anything, she had said the wrong thing. Coral was doing that thing with her lips where they smooshed about on her face as though she wanted to speak but couldn't.

If she had something to say, just get on with it already. It had been an exhausting day in what was the most troubling week of an abysmal lifetime. Hadn't she suffered enough throughout countless days? In her youth, Helicant grinned and reveled in the so-called consequences of men. Nothing could be worse than the atrocities they'd already committed, but she was so dreadfully wrong. But even in her numerous years, Helicant could've never guessed that, for once in the history of Christianity, their God actually listened.

Coral, of course, was oblivious to anything apart from her own neutral existence in Helicant's mind.

"Destiny is in her room. It's the west wing on the third floor. First door on the right. It's the only hall without a floor runner. Feel free to check with her. Might urge her to move it along."

She let out a sigh of relief as Coral gave a polite nod before leaving the room. Perhaps she'd get herself a whiskey, but then Edward would come sniffing like a bloodhound. The punch would serve.

The juice was a pink lemonade of sorts. It was the perfect amount of sour and sweet and a tinge of bitter aftertaste. Helicant admitted her sister, annoying as she was, could produce delightful concoctions. They were all quite talented, her sisters. Not that they had any choice.

With Coral out of the way, Helicant seated herself by the fire and observed Carl and Daniel's chess match. Drew noticed Helicant and gave her a polite nod; she returned the acknowledgment.

Joseph stood over his father as if he were watching, but Helicant could see the way he lost interest. His eyes looked around when everyone else was enthralled with the game. Helicant smiled with the realization that Joseph didn't know how to play chess. Not that she knew either, but at least she didn't pretend.

"How fares the game?" she asked as she crossed her legs.

Edward and Joseph glanced her way, but the players remained un-moved. Daniel watched the board and took measure of every piece. Carl was wiping sweat off his balding head. "Daniel always makes a mockery of me at chess."

"He's quite the prodigy," Edward said. "I was never able to defeat Carl in chess growing up."

"Yes, and since this one learned, I've yet to recover my dignity," Carl quipped.

"He is good," Drew said.

Daniel smirked but refused to allow the praise to sink in.

To see a man and his son connect in such a loving, gentle way made her smile. She approved of this boy whole-heartedly; she only hoped Destiny felt the same way.

Edward was leaning against the mantle as though it were a lifeline. His glass was once again full. How did he manage that? She hid the decanter in a secret cupboard in the bookcase. How could he know about it and sneak a refill without her seeing it?

What was more peculiar than his ability to sniff out any alcohol within a mile was his impressively long fingernails. Helicant had to struggle to keep from saying something out loud. They were thick and sharp, almost claw-like. Rather unsanitary for a good doctor. Helicant tore her sights away before it became rudely apparent.

He was staring at the wolf on the mantel as if he were deeply contemplating its existence in his drunken stupor.

"Makes you wish you and William had a son?" Edward asked, nodding to Daniel.

Normally, she wouldn't play into his musings, but she felt inexplicably safe, and her tongue was willing to express as much. "I'm surprised Beth didn't want more."

"She did," Edward said. "We tried, but nothing ever came of it. Sometimes it's not meant to be."

There was no point to this conversation. Everyone on the island knew it was their duty to produce as many children as possible. Unfortunately, the population was the extent of their possibilities. She'd gone over the lineage with Sophie many times to root out the cause. The Sallows family seldom had stillbirths, but they also seldom conceived.

Destiny was a miracle. Born to Helicant at the unsuspecting age of fifty-four. The twins were just as astonishing. For a brief time, everyone prayed to the gods for twins, thinking it possible. She couldn't mourn for her family. It was all Helicant could do to ensure the survival of the only one untouched by the curse.

"My sister has a different version of events." Helicant waded through the saccharin sweetness that dulled the ache and clouded her mind.

Drew jerked his eyes upward but recovered, not wanting to be seen as an interested party. Helicant no longer cared who heard. Her head drooped on her neck, and her feet floated like she was soaking in lukewarm water. Her head dug into the couch, and she waited for Edward's next move.

He was staring into the fire now. The glass of whiskey emitted an amber glow as it swirled around in the tumbler. For a moment, it seemed that he had lost all interest in the drink, but then his fingers twitched, once again prompted for a sip.

"William didn't strike me as the most romantic man."

"On the contrary," Helicant said. "He was a wonderful husband."

Edward's grip on the glass was threatening the integrity of the glassware. The pads of his fingers turned white as he pressed against it. Helicant wanted to drive home the point that her late husband was not up for discussion.

"William was a most affectionate and loyal man. He was the sort of man I could always rely on. Trustworthy."

Edward's glass broke in his hand, startling everyone from the chess game. "I'm so sorry, Helicant. These glasses are so frail in their old age."

"Are you hurt?" Drew was on his feet and ready to aid his father.

Flexing his hand in the firelight, there wasn't a single scratch on his soft hands. Did no one else notice Edward's unsightly fingernails or the hirsute patches on the tops of his hands?

"Not at all. How lucky is that?"

"It's no trouble," Helicant said as she stood. "Those glasses are as old as the house. I'll grab a broom from the basement."

"Do you need any help," Daniel asked. He too was now standing. It occurred to her that he stood because the lady of the house was standing. What a respectful boy.

"No, young man, I am quite fine. Finish your game."

Helicant turned to give Edward one last hard grin before closing the pocket door of the drawing room as if to say Checkmate.

The happenings in the kitchen were just as interesting as they were in the drawing room. Helicant could hear Beth's compelling story of the mutant stuffed rabbit and was surprised to find that there was something interesting about Coral after all.

Sophie did not seem to find the story nearly as hilarious as she did. Her sister had taken the brunt of Beth's verbal barrage long enough, and her patience had waned by the time Helicant reached the swinging doors of the kitchen.

When she came into the room, Helicant bit back a gasp. The kitchen was a disaster. She spent all morning scrubbing the floors and cleaning the cookware. In a matter of a few hours, everything was covered in dust, cobwebs, and what appeared to be food bits. She was careful not to give her shock away, but had the twins gone blind?

Helicant blamed the louder twin for the oversight. She understood how taxing Beth's nature could be. Poor Sophie was likely so overwhelmed by her sister's gossip that she probably rushed through cleaning to escape. That and Sophie's eyes were not what they used to be.

She could hear footprints plodding from the backdoor. Beth was returning to the kitchen, and the unproductive mayhem would continue. Something caught Helicant's eye as it dripped from the ceiling. How did they manage to get potato peels on the ceiling, of all things?

No, enough was enough.

"You are to blame as much as she. You've become far too accustomed to living in silence, but unlike you, she is truly alone. Her husband and son despise her, as do her sisters. She has no one."

Beth stood in the doorway, privy to the gossip firsthand.

It wasn't always fun to be the bad guy. Beth's eyes were large and amassing tears as she dropped a basket of eggs on the stone floor. Helicant winced at the cracking shells. Yet another mess.

Sophie tried to run after their sister, but Helicant stopped her. It was too late in the evening for this. At the rate the twins were going, the family wouldn't make it to dinner.

In all the chaos, she almost forgot what she had come to the kitchen for. Clearly, there was no broom in this room. If there had been, Sophie might have had incentive to use it. Without another word, she left the kitchen and proceeded to wander aimlessly around her own home, searching for a broom. The next likely place for it would be the dining room.

Perhaps Abigail was using it.

Beth

She couldn't go stomping around the grounds of Sallows Hall forever.

Mist unfurled from the forest and was crawling to the lawn. The night chill would follow soon after. What precious few hours of daylight they had were wasted in the kitchen. Beth kicked at the chickens that were slow to get out of her way.

Who died and made Helicant boss? Well, it was their parents who died and made her the matron. Mother and father had her and Sophie much later in life. She supposed it gave Helicant a sense of responsibility that a sibling closer in age wouldn't.

Mother was in her fifties when she had her and her sister. Their father was in his thirties at the time. He was just a boy when they got pregnant with Helicant. Betrothed before he could even walk. It wasn't always the families who decided who married; sometimes, there was little option. Her parents were coupled by the island itself.

Beth knew it was wrong to wander around and sulk. This wasn't about her. Destiny was a good girl, if not a little curious; she deserved to be happy on this day. Beth went back to the kitchen, treading through the back door to find Sophie still hard at work.

"Do you need me to do anything?"

Sophie rushed to her and embraced her in a hug. "I'm so sorry, Beth."

"Our sister has a sharp tongue."

"I should have just said something," Sophie said, pulling her to arm's length. "You forget I live by myself. I'm not used to so much talking."

Her twin looked less and less like her as the years went on. Her hair was long and kept in a single braid. Her face sagged more, and Beth could tell by the way she got around the kitchen that Sophie couldn't see as well as she once did.

It was all that damned reading. She told Helicant as much, but no one ever listened to her.

Beth shook her head. "I talk too much. It gets the better of me."

"I could still use your help," Sophie offered. "The food is nearly done, but I don't want to leave Helicant this mess. Why don't you serve in the dining room while I take care of things here?"

Sophie knew Beth hated doing dishes and understood her need to be seen. This was a peace offering, and Beth was happy to agree. "We still have an engagement to witness."

The sisters went up to the drawing room to wait for the special moment. Everyone was there except for Destiny and Abigail. Coral was in the midst of updating Helicant on Destiny's status.

"Abigail is doing her hair," Coral said with no small sense of importance.

Helicant cocked her head and narrowed her eyes. "I would have thought Abigail relieved of duty with your arrival."

Poor Coral. Her smooth, fair skin was growing pink around the cheeks. "Destiny insisted on having Abigail with her."

What Coral was really saying was that Destiny didn't want her there. Helicant understood as much and gave a nod. "They are close. It's only natural that Destiny wants her support."

Coral lingered in the matron's path, unwilling to leave without some token of approval. She didn't understand this about Helicant, but the matron didn't hand out compliments, nor did she require them. Beth pressed her lips together and watched as their sister-in-law made a fool of herself. Helicant tilted her head as if trying to ascertain what it was to be human.

Beth decided to throw Coral a line. She stepped beside Helicant and said, "It was good of you to check on them and to give Helicant an update. God knows those girls would have gotten distracted if not for you."

Coral practically melted with relief. Upon seeing the reaction, Helicant also chimed in, "If Destiny has her way, she'll come in here wearing those ugly boots."

"Yes, she tried to put those on."

"Good gods," Helicant said. "You didn't let her?"

Coral shook her head. "Absolutely not. It's bad enough that Abigail is wearing them, but you can't tell that girl anything."

"I suppose it's better than running around barefoot like we used to," Beth said.

All three women stared off and nodded. They all remembered the days they worked for someone's wedding, funeral, or other special engagement. In their youth, there was a decline in livestock. Without leather, they cleaned the house barefoot, the cold, hard floors unyielding to their feet.

Daniel silently placed his rook into a checkmate, and Carl bowed his head. The boy was clever, always borrowing this book and that from her collection. She didn't mind because he always returned them. Beth was about to congratulate Daniel but halted at the sight of Carl.

His handkerchief was sagging from the weight of accumulated moisture. Sweat dripped from his fingers, and his shirt clung to him as though someone dumped a pitcher of water over his head. She hoped he wasn't feverish. Beth tried many times to get Edward's attention, but he was either too drunk to notice or too drunk to care.

"Is Carl all right?" Beth asked.

Coral turned back to inspect her husband the way a woman would for a small child before rolling her eyes. "I don't know who's more nervous, Carl or Daniel."

"Well done, my boy!" Carl cheered. "If you'll excuse me for a moment."

Carl pardoned himself from the room, and Coral trailed behind.

Helicant didn't look at her; her sister's eyes were fixed on Edward. Beth was unsure of what was going on in her sister's mind, but she didn't like it. "Carl is the sort of man who would try to push through, isn't he?"

"He is kind."

"It's a shame he's so unattractive." Beth's mouth dropped when her sister said that. Helicant wasn't one to hold back, but she seemed out of sorts tonight.

"Are you feeling well?"

"Perfectly," Helicant said, but Beth couldn't dismiss her sister's glassy eyes and drooping posture.

Helicant went to the punch bowl and helped herself to the punch. She was glad Helicant enjoyed it. Beth seated herself beside Joseph and Drew while Edward challenged Daniel to a round of Chess.

Joseph swore under his breath as he blinked vacantly at the ceiling. Poor lad. He was a young man in his prime, forced to live on an island with little to do. The Sallows gift was also their curse. Beth had long lost interest in exploring beyond the island, but when she was Joseph's age, she too struggled with remaining on an island for the sake of long-forgotten myths.

"How are you holding up, Jo?" Beth asked.

Joseph shrugged. With his mother gone, he was free to relax. With an elbow on the table, he rested his head on his palm. "Just waiting for it to be over."

"When I was nine, I had to attend my great aunt's funeral. The woman was ninety-seven and bedridden for most of my life. I'd never even met her. The funeral was the most boring experience of my life. At some point, I was so frustrated with sitting and listening to old people talk that I started crying."

Joseph released a laugh from the belly. At least someone didn't mind her stories.

"Except I couldn't make a fuss, so I just sat there with tears rolling down my face. Everyone thought I was crying over my great aunt that no one chastised me."

"At least no one told you how selfish you were being," Joseph said.

"This island isn't fair to anyone, especially not young folk. Your parents were a lucky exception. Most of us never find happiness."

Drew had his back turned and was watching the game, but Beth imagined he was listening too. Joseph sipped his punch and said, "I just wish there were more of us or that the island was bigger."

"If it were bigger, I doubt the king of England would have given it up so easily. He'd send the whole British Navy if it were a good size."

"But instead, he sent one little family to defeat the monsters," Joseph said without enthusiasm. "You'd think he'd at least send a few families."

"Who would agree to live on an island that wasn't theirs?"

Joseph nodded. "I suppose that's true."

"They never intended us to carry on this long, that's why." Drew joined in on the conversation.

That had never occurred to her. What a morbid assessment. Their ancestors came here—seventeen people in all. They had made a deal with the King of England. The family would eradicate the monsters that emerged from the island, and in exchange, they would be the sole owners of the island. To live in any manner they wished, without the crown or taxation.

The original family came here with all the materials to build Sallows Hall, where they all lived together. They built catacombs beneath the house to contain the monsters. They built this house with the intent of growing and flourishing. It never occurred to Beth that they were never meant to survive here after all this time.

"Don't be so morbid," Edward grumbled.

Drew stretched his large frame and crossed his arms. "From what I've read on monarchs and taxation, they'd rather us be dead than to forego taxes."

"Taxes," Beth scoffed. "What an absurd notion. Paying someone you don't know for things another person uses."

"It's not all that different than what we do here on the island," Daniel said. "My mother doesn't pay for doctor visits because she makes the clothes that are on his back. Drew doesn't charge my father for the meat he hunts because my father repaired your roof just recently. You make medicine even though no one pays you because we all contribute to the social good. Taxes are the way for everyone to contribute to the welfare of all."

"What a well-thought-out statement, Daniel," Helicant observed from her stupor. If she didn't know better, Beth swore that Helicant was trying to give the boy confidence.

"Of course, there are flaws in taxation," Daniel said. "Sometimes the people who decide what the taxes are used on don't have the common good in mind. On a much smaller scale like ours, things work out nicely, but when on a large scale, it's easy to mismanage."

Beth had to admit that Daniel was brilliant. Joseph, on the other hand, was staring blankly into the fire. Abigail the doctor and Daniel a scholar of sorts, yet if Joseph had any ambition or interest, she couldn't find it. Drew stood up, poured punch into cups, and began handing them out. Once everyone had a cup, he raised his in the air.

"A toast to the future leader of the island and his bride-to-be."

"No," Helicant corrected. "To the future leader and her groom-to-be."

Drew nodded, accepting the correction. "A toast to the future matron and her groom."

Everyone raised their glasses and drank. Drew took a sip, whereas Edward drank his down greedily, encouraging Joseph to do the same. Not to be shown up, Helicant did the same, and Beth went along with it.

Only Daniel and Drew had punch remaining.

Coral

Coral brought her husband to the bathroom and helped him out of his jacket and vest. His black shirt was drenched in a cold sweat. "Oh my god, Carl."

"I don't know what's wrong with me," he said, staring down at his chest. It already had a new layer of sheen.

She placed a hand on his forehead. "No sign of fever."

"I don't feel feverish," he said. "In fact, I feel wonderful."

This couldn't be normal. She was at a loss for what to do. "Maybe I should fetch Edward and—"

Carl waved the idea off. "I don't want to disturb anyone. Besides, what could he possibly do?"

Her eyes scanned him for any indication of distress. There was none to be found, and even if there was, what could she do? She couldn't bear the thought of losing her husband. He was her quiet rock. Her encouragement. They'd been inseparable since they were children, and when her parents conspired to marry her to the older, more established doctor, she fled and hid in the forest for days. It was Carl who found her in the cave and her father who relented.

Tears began to form in her eyes, and Carl pulled her in close. "It's all right, silly girl."

Coral gave a few deliberate sniffs. Mostly because she was crying but also because she noticed something unusual. "You don't smell like perspiration. Not like body odor at all."

"Thank God for that." Carl laughed. Even in the highly unusual situation, his mood remained jolly.

"You smell like... Well, like water."

Not just any water. Specifically, the water in the fountain. At some point, one of their ancestors, only Sophie would know who, sculpted a fountain out of the chalky stone found by the cliffs. A hedge maze was built around it, and that maze consisted of their entertainment in their youth. She and Sophie used to love running through the maze as teens. Her brother William would often chase them through it.

Even in their younger years, Sophie had already read every scrap of history she could find. "It's from the old well. Corrupted some time ago, so they turned it into a fountain."

"Why does it smell so strange? Like aloe and...anise?" Coral leaned in closer to inhale a little bit deeper. Sophie didn't seem nearly as interested. She had her sights set on William. Leaning in a little closer, she thought perhaps...

"Boo!" William's voice boomed from behind her.

Coral jumped and swung her arm out instinctively, swatting at her brother. He was a young man in his twenties then. Blond and strapping in his woolen jacket and trousers. His green eyes were striking. She cried when Daniel inherited those electric eyes.

If only Destiny could see how beautiful he was.

"Perhaps it's just too hot under all those clothes. I think I shall take a walk." Carl said, pulling her from the memory.

"Without a shirt on? Coral objected.

"Are you wearing an undershirt, my dear?"

Coral laughed, but it was a solution. She turned around, and Carl helped her unbutton her dress. The exchange was made, and Carl was wearing her white linen undershirt. "I'm going to stroll around the gardens. I don't want to draw attention. If I'm not back, just assume I went home."

"You're going to miss Daniel's wedding?"

Carl grinned through it, but Coral knew he was disappointed. "We'll always be together."

She watched her husband leave the bathroom. There was nothing more she could do for him, and their son needed them now.

Just as she was coming out of the bathroom, the echo of a scream sounded from downstairs.

Straining to hear better, she tensed as the wails of pain grew louder. They were coming from the kitchen. Her heart pounded in alarm. Sophie.

Lifting her skirts, Coral sped down the stairs and into the main entryway.

"Sophie?" She cried.

Coral didn't wait to hear a response. She ran through the swing doors and ran squarely into the woman in the kitchen. Whatever she was holding fell to the floor. The dish crashed into the stone floor and shattered. Molten hot mashed potatoes splattered in every direction.

"Oh," Sophie said as she sat up. "What happened?"

Coral looked around in bewilderment. "I heard someone scream-ing."

Sophie groaned. "This will be the third time I'll be cleaning the kitchen today."

"Sophie, I'm so sorry. I heard a woman wailing in pain. I was worried something had happened to you."

"I wasn't screaming. No one has been here besides me."

She caused all this ruckus over nothing. Still, the screaming was so loud, it was a wonder no one else heard it. Must've been those weird pipes along the bathroom walls groaning in futility. Who truly thought indoor plumbing would actually work? It was a waste of piping.

"Why don't you take a break? I'll clean this up and remake the potatoes. I need something to take my mind off Carl anyhow."

"It will go faster if I help." Sophie's face was so drawn and haggard. Coral truly regretted running into her the way she did.

"Beth is in the drawing room. Send her down."

Sophie was unable to resist. "All right," she said as she threw off her apron. "I love that punch Beth makes."

Coral smiled. While she had made a mess of things, she came at precisely the right moment. She found the mop and bucket in the small entryway that led to the back door. The potatoes had cooled quickly against the stone floor, so it took little time to scoop them into the bucket. A wheelbarrow just outside the kitchen door was used to dispose of leftovers for big events like this. Sophie's pigs would eat well tonight.

By the time Coral started mopping, Beth was downstairs. Of course, she wanted to know every detail of what happened. "Sophie doesn't tell me anything," she complained.

"We ran into each other. I rushed in too quickly."

"Why rush into the kitchen at all?"

"Oh, I thought I heard something. I think this engagement party has gotten the better of me."

Beth took up the tin pale of potatoes and set to scrubbing. "Everyone is out of sorts tonight."

Once the mopping was done, Coral joined Beth, and together, they scrubbed and peeled the potatoes.

"Has she even come down yet?" Coral asked.

Beth only shook her head.

Maybe Destiny's problems were worse than any of them realized. What if she said no? Coral had been under the assumption that Destiny was going to say yes. No one would go to all this effort for a farce engagement. Then again, she didn't know Helicant very well.

When the matron came to their door, offering marriage between Daniel and Destiny, it was a dream come true. The livestock had better accommodations than their tiny hovel at this point. It wasn't fair that the largest family had to cram into a two-bedroom cottage.

Side by side, Coral and Beth paired potatoes. She hoped it wouldn't take too long. Not only did she want to be there when Daniel proposed, but she wanted to spend as little time as she could alone with Beth.

"Careful," Beth warned. "You go too fast, and you'll cut yourself."

Coral gave a weak smile, and Beth nodded. "They won't start without you. Daniel needs you there. Helicant knows that."

She didn't want to admit it, but Beth's words were comforting. "I know so little about Helicant."

"She's got a harsh tone and a stony demeanor, but she is fiercely protective and intuitive. She wouldn't do anything to you that she wouldn't want done to her unless it comes to Destiny." Beth's laugh bounced off the walls. "She'll murder you if you upset Destiny."

Coral took a deep breath and quieted her thoughts. "Like most parents then."

Beth set aside a potato and picked up another. "It must be hard having a daughter. So many things I don't need to worry about."

"They are different," Coral said, picking up a new potato. "Boys and girls. Of course, there comes a point where you can't control either."

"That is true. You can't stop them from making mistakes. They seem determined to make them no matter what you say."

"Drew seems to have found his niche," Coral pointed. "He's a skilled hunter. Must take after his father."

"In more ways than one." Beth agreed. What could she mean by that? Before she could respond, Beth dug up a large potato and scrapped away at it. "Daniel is the brightest young man. Helicant is beyond impressed with him. I think we all are."

Coral flushed with the praise. "He's always been that way. So patient with his brother, and he's always kind to Abigail."

"He's a true gentleman, then."

Something about Beth's tone just then made her pause and look at Beth. "What does that mean?"

Beth shrugged. "Abigail refuses to marry. You must wonder why that is."

Coral's potato slipped from her hand, and she had no intention of searching the water for another. "I admit I had hoped she'd marry. Maybe one day she will change her mind, but Abigail is going to be the next doctor. She's quite accomplished, even if it's not the way I imagined for her. Besides, had you allowed her to stay with you while she interned with Edward, she might have had a chance to get to know Drew better."

Beth was searching the water herself, but it seemed there was nothing to be found. "I don't think it's Drew she wanted to get better acquainted with."

There she had it. Turning to face Beth, she stared the woman down. Her hand found the sewing kit in her pocket, and her fingers worked it until she loosened a needle. It pricked her in retaliation.

Rumors had circled for the years about Abigail and Edward, but she didn't know whether to believe them. She never had the opportunity to call it out until now.

"Oh, dear," Beth said slowly. "I don't know why I would say such a thing."

"Have you seen them acting inappropriately?" Coral asked.

"No," Beth said. Her eyes were heavy-lidded. Had she been drinking?

"Has anyone seen them acting...acquainted?"

Beth shook her head. It was something that had hung over her for such a long time. Abigail hadn't slept with Edward, from what anyone had seen or heard. The rumors were just that, fabrications. And the one who made such rumors was the woman beside her, fishing potatoes from the murky water.

Beth tried to mutter a defense, but it was no use. Coral got within an inch of her cousin's face and glared at her. Heat rose from her throat and crept along her skin. The weight of the sewing kit weighed like a stone in her pocket.

A brief vision of sticking one of her taxidermy pins straight into Beth's eye. "If you ever spread rumors about my daughter again, I'll sew your mouth shut."

Storming out of the room, she left Beth to drunkenly tend to her potatoes.

Those remaining in the drawing room were also out of sorts. Daniel and Drew faced off at the chess board as if they were about to brawl. She hesitated to even speak up, the tension was so tightly wound. Any joy or mirth left with Carl.

Helicant was in a daze of sorts. She was lying in her chair in a most informal manner, her legs spread as she was hunched into the chair. Sitting beside the punch bowl, Sophie didn't use the ladle; she simply dipped her cup into the bowl and carried on drinking. Edward, too, was lulling in a corner chair, circling the rim of his cup with a lazy finger.

"Hello, everyone."

"Where's Father?" Daniel asked.

Coral had nearly forgotten that Carl had left, and the guilt of telling Daniel his father was unwell clung tighter than her collar. "Your father wasn't feeling well. I sent him home."

"He was sweating rather profusely."

It was obvious that Carl was ailing. Hopefully, he'd recover soon. She couldn't think about what would happen if he didn't.

"Would you like a glass of punch?" Drew asked her; he was already getting up to get a glass for her. "Come, sit here."

"Thank you, Drew." She sat down beside Daniel, and Drew gave her a glass of punch. Joseph was half asleep against the wall, and Edward was sitting opposite Helicant, staring into the fire. In the bride's delay, everyone had grown sleepy. This didn't bode well. Not that she expected the nuptials to be a spectacle, but she had hoped it would be a happy affair. This wasn't exactly happy.

"My sister is finishing the potatoes?" Sophie asked.

Just the mention of Beth sent her skin prickling. "She is."

If Sophie thought it strange that Coral would offload the work she volunteered to do, she didn't show it. Besides, she deserved to be with her son at this time. He was the groom, after all.

DESTINY

Destiny's vision went narrow as she made her way down the stairs. Her sweaty hand slipped across the railing as she gasped helplessly for air. She tried to do so quietly so as to not alert Abigail, but not fainting and falling down the stairs took priority.

Then again, if she slipped and fell, rolled down the harrowing stairs, and broke her neck, Destiny would never be afraid again.

Her cousin looped her arm into Destiny's free arm and helped her. Destiny tripped on her dress and let out a startled "oh," followed by a giggle.

"Just one flight of stairs and a nod," Abigail promised. "That's all you need to do, and this will all be over."

The proposal would be over, but the marriage would begin. What would he expect from her? Sharing a bedroom was out of the question, though Mother said that she and father slept separately. They'd take meals together at the opposite ends of the dining room, so that wouldn't be so bad. She'd have someone to talk to other than her mother. There were perks to being married—if she could manage to say yes.

It all felt so stupid, but at the heart of her anxiety, there was pressure to perform. To be like her mother. Only she wasn't her mother. Destiny didn't want to make decisions for an entire island. Imagine her telling people what to do when she couldn't walk down a flight of stairs by herself.

Before she could turn and run, Abigail slid open the door and pulled Destiny into a room filled with everyone who inhabited the island. All staring at her. Expecting something from her.

She couldn't breathe, and her legs wobbled like undercooked pudding.

No one bothered to stand when they saw her except for him.

Daniel kept his eyes lowered. She hadn't seen him since the night terrors started. How could someone be so unchanged yet changed at the same time? He was nearly as tall as Drew. Daniel always had dark hair, but it was thick and shaggy around his face. His fringe hovered over his eyes as though he'd intentionally grown it out just for her. But beneath all that, he was still the same boy she knew all those years ago.

He was at a chessboard with Drew. Destiny's ribs railed against her corset. She needed to relax if she wanted to breathe, but her heart hammered between her ears. Every nerve twitched like it was on fire and urged her to flee. Escape. Run.

Dread...

Abigail led her into the room, and for a horrible moment, Daniel looked her in the eyes, and her heart palpitated so hard she thought it was going to stop. No longer able to focus on breathing, Destiny tried to turn and run, but Abigail held fast and whispered, "You're almost there."

Destiny heard her mother's voice, but it seemed strange. Hollow and gruff. "Let's get on with it. I think we're all ready for dinner."

"Are you sure we shouldn't—" Daniel began to argue.

"You have the ring. Let's be done with all of this."

Destiny was starting to cry. She didn't want to cry in front of everyone. She wanted to leave. Biting the knuckle of her free hand, she tried to distract herself as Daniel kneeled. To his credit, he avoided eye contact as he pulled forth the ruby ring and presented it to her. All the same, Destiny needed to protect herself by looking away.

"Destiny," he started. "I know you're frightened. I am, too. Just look at my hand. Go on."

Despite her eyes jerking this way and that, she managed to find his hand. It trembled harder than her own. He was every bit frightened, but he took no shame in it. The room around her stilled, and something like peace warmed in her heart. She wasn't alone in this.

"Daniel..."

"It's scary business, getting married. I don't know what's going to happen any more than you do. I know you're afraid of my eyes, but I also know that you don't like that. I can't promise you'll never not be afraid, but what I can promise is that you'll be the one to decide what you need, and I will support you. I've read a lot about phobias, and it's something we can overcome. Worst case scenario, I can just wear a blindfold for the rest of my life. I really don't mind."

Destiny was openly weeping. He said the most perfect thing anyone could ever say. She didn't notice it, but she was breathing normally, and her vision had restored enough to notice her entire family was slouched around the drawing room.

No one expected anything from her. They were just tired and likely hungry.

"I..." she stammered. "I... Yes."

She had said it. Destiny had said yes. Not to her mother's wishes or Abigail's fantasies. Not to Coral's ambition or to spite Drew. She had said yes to Daniel. If there was one thing she knew, it was that Daniel was indeed the right person for her.

"It is done," her mother said. "They are now married."

Abigail erupted in sobs, and everyone was sort of applauding. It was a confused and lazy applause, but that didn't matter. She and Daniel were married.

There was supposed to be more. A binding of the hands and vows, but she was grateful to omit such things. They could always perform that ceremony later.

Daniel, so shocked by the answer, his eyes met hers. It was just an instant, but Destiny's body went rigid. Saliva pooled in the throat she couldn't swallow.

"Sorry," he said. "I just really didn't expect that."

Her heart bolted from her chest and seized.

Green eyes full of rage and despair of a monster who screamed for her. Begged for her. What did he want? Before she could ask, he plunged a spike into his own face to dull the pain. Destiny's knees knocked together. Someone was holding her up, but the room went sideways.

"She needs air," Edward's voice came through the fog.

Destiny's sight came back into focus. She was lying on a loveseat in the downstairs lavatory. Abigail? It was her mother who was seated beside her.

"You're okay," Mother cooed.

Destiny sat up, the mobility in her waist restored. She noted the corset was hanging on the changing screen. "That corset was too small. Abigail couldn't have known that. I know she took her time lacing it."

"I have no doubt that it exacerbated your condition," Helicant said.

"The party," Destiny started. She was afraid that she ruined the party.

"Still going. Everyone is getting ready for dinner. Daniel is quite worried, but you're not the first lady to faint from a poorly fit corset while being proposed to."

"I'm going down to the basement for some wine," Helicant said. "Come with me."

Her biggest worry was that she'd faint in front of everyone, and she did, but it wasn't a big deal. Expected even, given that she was wearing a corset.

Destiny walked through the kitchen with her mother to find Sophie getting the food ready for the dumbbell waiter. Sophie turned and smiled. "Congratulations!"

Destiny smiled and rubbed her arms, but she was happy. "Thanks."

"I'm getting a bottle of wine from the basement," Helicant told Sophie.

"Better make it two. You know Edward."

Helicant rolled her eyes. "I'll hide the bottle opener in the basement."

She was at the back door and found herself craving the fresh night air. A chill to remind her that Destiny wasn't dreaming. She was a married woman.

"I'm going to step outside."

Helicant waved her off as she made her way into the basement. Destiny figured that meant she didn't care. Her mother was more concerned about how to keep the wine out of Edward's hands. Sophie was humming as she moved around dishes and plates. Destiny couldn't help but laugh at how excited her aunt was.

Beth came wadding into the kitchen with half-eaten trays of food. "Help me clear the drawing room."

Everyone was happy and humming along, eager for dinner. It felt like the perfect time to slip out for a bit of solace. Padding to the patio, just outside the hedge maze, Destiny sat with her hands between her legs and took in the cold. It was well past four. Dinner was going to be later than her mother anticipated, but at least she was married.

That was the goal of the evening. Destiny raked her hands through her hair. The whole thing still felt unreal; she scarcely remembered agreeing, but the ruby ring on her hand served as a weighty reminder.

There was a click of a door, and Destiny turned to find Drew. He had two glasses of pink punch. She wasn't out here very long. Beth must have given away her whereabouts. Destiny's eyes fell awkwardly to the ground. He wasn't the man she wanted to see.

"I wanted to congratulate you," Drew said, sitting a cup before her.

Destiny always felt odd around Drew. He smiled when people were rude to him, and he spent a lot of time by himself in the woods. And she never learned why he made random visits to her house at night. She supposed they all had their eccentricities.

"Thank you," Destiny said, reaching for the cup. "Are you next?"

Drew let out a hearty laugh as he sat in the chair and crossed a leg over one knee. "Abigail and I... It's complicated."

Rather than respond, Destiny drank the punch.

"She has goals," Drew said. "Brilliant ones. I support her in that, even if others do not. Someone needs to be skilled in medicine when my father hits the bucket. I don't mind waiting if it means she accomplishes her goals."

Maybe underneath that cocky attitude was a good man after all. "I wish her mother acknowledged Abigail's talents the way you do."

Drew's lips peeled away from his teeth with a grin, but it looked menacing somehow. Like a wolf baring its fangs. With the evening coming, the light was playing tricks with her eyes.

"You took that down rather quickly. You must be parched. Here, take mine."

"Oh no…"

"I insist."

She was thirsty. The sour punch didn't seem to change that, but Destiny felt far more relaxed than she had in weeks. Her feet felt as though they were floating. She giggled before taking his cup, though she couldn't quite understand why.

"Her mother just wants out of that shed she calls a home. I can't blame her. The thing is crumbling faster than Carl can repair it. It would be easier to maintain this behemoth if more people lived in it too," Drew said, motioning to Sallows Hall.

"I think there's more to it than that."

Drew's eyes narrowed. "I suppose there's no reason to hide it from you. You're a grown woman. There have been rumors for quite some time that Abigail and my father…"

"No!" Destiny clutched the glass between her fingers. "I don't believe that for a moment."

Drew gave a single nod. "My mother does. And when my mother thinks something, the whole island will hear about it. He has admitted to infidelity to my mother, though he refused to name the woman."

She didn't know that about Edward. It shouldn't have changed her opinion of the doctor, but Destiny felt the tinges of an upset stomach. "I had no idea."

"You can see what an awkward position that puts me in," Drew said. "My father may have seduced the only woman on the island I expressed interest in."

Destiny didn't know what to think of that. Edward was always so kind to her. Mother never seemed to like his presence; this must have been why.

"I'm sorry. I didn't realize Edward was that sort of man."

"He's a dog," Drew hissed. "He hounds after any woman he can. When did he first start fucking you?"

Bile surged up her throat. Crude and wrong. She wanted to leave, but her limbs were slow and doughy. Moving her head from side to side, everything felt so clumsy. Had Drew put something in the punch?

"He's quite protective of you. He even threatened me. At first, I believed the rumors about him and Abigail, but with the two of you in the same room, all became clear. He doesn't care about Abigail at all. It's you."

Destiny shook her head in denial. Drew was wrong, very wrong, about her. Edward had never touched her. The smug look on Drew's face told her that the truth didn't matter. He wanted to hurt his father, and she was nothing but a casualty.

"I can't wait to see the look on his face when I tell him that I've fucked you too."

With all the speed and power she could muster, Destiny pushed her heavy body from the chair with her arms and bolted into the maze. He was fast. Drew nearly caught her at the entrance, but she knew of a hedge with weak branches a few bushes in and lunged for it.

This was her home, and she had spent many days lost in the maze.

There were several shortcuts she had made for herself over the years that only she knew about. Once she lost him in the maze, she'd run back to the house for help. Expose the vile man for what he was.

Destiny rounded a corner only to find Drew right behind her. She sprang forth again, this time taking a dead end with another secret door that would take her closer to the end of the maze. She could hear Drew laughing as he searched for the same opening.

"You're like a little doe," he shouted. "I hope you kick like that when you're mounted."

Destiny felt like vomiting, but she couldn't afford to slow down. Her legs were already sluggish from whatever he put in her punch, and she wasn't the most athletically inclined to begin with. Already panting hard, she was certain it gave her away.

The center of the maze opened before her, surrounding her with choices. She could double back using her secret entrances and hope Drew didn't catch on. She could take the shortcut to the end of the maze. It would be the farthest away from the house, but Destiny could potentially lose him. If she took the side hedge, it would be hardest to discover her whereabouts, but at this point she had no idea where he was, and she could end up running into her would-be rapist.

It was a gamble, but Destiny took the shortcut through the side near the tree. She had made it when she was eleven and didn't think anyone else knew about it.

"Destiny!" Drew called in a mocking tone.

He was in the center of the maze. At some point, her cousin learned the maze, too. That line about Edward was bullshit. He had all of this planned before the party even started. Perhaps Edward's "threats" served to confirm his desires, but this was all premeditated.

She zigzagged through the maze. His footfalls were so quiet, making it impossible to determine his whereabouts, but he'd occasionally call out her name to taunt her. Forcing her way through a bush, Destiny heard the crunch of someone walking. She held her breath as Drew sauntered by.

"Destiny!" he called. "Come on, silly girl."

With only a patchwork of Drew's figure through the hedge, she could see him, but he couldn't see her in the shadows. She thanked the gods above for the choice of color the Sallows wore to celebrate.

Destiny steeled her nerves and waited for Drew to wander further away.

She remained there in total silence until his voice called to her from a safer distance. Her knees were weakening, and her stomach threatened to rebel. Destiny didn't have much time. She needed to get somewhere safe.

"Destiny?" a different male voice called.

She didn't wait for Drew to form a new strategy. Destiny snaked her way out of the side exit and rushed to Daniel's arms. His eyes caught hers, but it was too dark for her to see the color.

"Daniel!"

He didn't ask what was happening or why she was so upset. Wordlessly, Daniel scooped her up and ran towards the mansion without delay. She wrapped her arms around his neck, buried her face into his shoulder, and sobbed—leaving Drew somewhere still inside the maze.

BETH

Beth had just cleared the last of the dishes in the drawing room. Joseph was fast asleep with his back against the wall in the drawing room. Edward was pacing. His glass empty, her husband seemed to lose all interest. Coral was fidgeting with something in her pocket as she stared out the window.

"I wish I knew if Carl had gone home or not," Coral said. "I suppose he did since he didn't come back."

Edward didn't seem to hear her; he, too, was fretting about something. This was the most miserable wedding she had ever attended. Everyone was so wrapped up in their own troubles, no one cared what the bride and groom did. They hadn't even done the vows. Was it even official without the hand-binding ceremony?

Daniel and Destiny were married. They could all move on to the fun part—wine and the food. Perhaps Edward was worried that Helicant wouldn't allow him to partake.

"Edward!" Daniel's voice echoed from downstairs. "We need the doctor."

Edward's eyes met hers. Something had happened, and without Abigail, she had to be ready. Beth gave him a reassuring nod. Whatever was happening, she would be by his side. Her husband led the way, and Beth followed. Coral followed her, leaving the beautiful sleeping boy in the drawing room.

Daniel was standing at the base of the stairs, Destiny in his arms like some sort of tragic romance depiction. The boy was terrified. His thick lower lip trembled. Edward sprinted down the stairs to their side.

"Did she faint again?" Edward asked.

Daniel shook his head. "We need to get her somewhere safe."

Edward checked her temperature and peered into her eyes, searching for signs of distress. "Can you stand, my dear?" he asked.

Destiny nodded, and Daniel gently lowered her legs to the ground, but he still held her around the waist as if he were afraid to let her go. Both men helped get Destiny to the restroom on the first floor. Edward monitored Destiny's movements, and she could tell by his furrowed brow that he was unhappy with what he was seeing.

Destiny lurched forward. A spray of vomit hit the floor. Edward glared accusingly at Daniel, but the boy was too concerned about his fiancé to care what Edward thought of him. Good boy. Don't let this become about what Edward thinks.

They got to the bathroom. Coral stood outside the door, watching from a safe distance. Daniel took a washcloth and patted at Destiny's face, all without directly looking at her in case it frightened her.

"What is going on?" Edward demanded.

"Beth said she went outside, so I went to look for her," Daniel said. "Only, she wasn't there. I heard Drew calling her name like he was taunting her. I called for her, and that's when she burst from the hedge maze. Jumped right into my arms."

"Destiny," Edward cupped the girl's head in his hands. Beth was worried for her but couldn't deny the twinge of jealousy. "Did you drink something you ought not to?"

"Punch," was all Destiny could get out.

"Her temperature is too low, and her pupils are oddly dilated. If I didn't know better, I'd say she's suffering from intoxication and exposure, but she wasn't outside that long."

"What do we do?" Daniel asked.

Edward straightened and searched the room. "Beth, she needs blankets, towels, anything."

"We should get her near the fire," she said.

Edward nodded. "That's good thinking."

She hated herself for it, but her heart swelled with her husband's praise. When was the last time he said something kind to her?

Edward moved to scoop up the girl, but Daniel was quicker. If she didn't know better, the two men were fighting over her. Why? Destiny, sick and her eyes unfocused, still reached for Daniel. Edward hovered near as they made their way up the stairs.

Poor Daniel huffed and puffed up each step, but he was determined to carry his wife. Beth ran back to the restroom for a pail in case Destiny was sick again. As she reached for the pale just beside the basin, the pipes that climbed the wall began to rattle violently.

"Good Lord," Beth muttered as she watched what seemed like something making its way through the pipe. They groaned and even buckled as something too large for them worked through the main tube. Rats maybe?

Entering the drawing room, she found Sophie kneeled beside Destiny. She was talking to the girl while Edward and Daniel were speaking in hushed tones in the corner. Edward's forehead was creased so hard. He glanced her way for a moment; was it pity in his eyes? He turned his back towards her so Beth could no longer observe their conversation. Coral was still staring out the window, fiddling with something in her pocket as though it were a talisman against evil.

"Where's Helicant?" she asked.

Everyone was so absorbed with what they were doing that they had all forgotten to alert Helicant that her daughter was ill. If Beth knew anything, it was that Helicant would tear through every single person in this room until she had answers.

Her sister would make Edward miserable until Destiny felt better. Perhaps it was best not to tell the matron just yet.

Beth noticed the pitcher of water beside Sophie's side. Sophie was coaxing Destiny into drinking as much as she could. Destiny complied with tiny sips. The poor girl. "I brought this from the bathroom, just in case."

"Oh good," Sophie said. "We might be needing that again."

Destiny's skin tone was improving. She was no longer cold to the touch, but she was still distraught. Her eyes were watery, and she was either unable or unwilling to speak. Destiny would stare into the fire for a few minutes before bursting into tears again.

Beth didn't like this. Whatever had happened to her went beyond sneaking into alcohol. Daniel didn't seem the sort to encourage a girl to be rendered helplessly intoxicated. Coral had been in the drawing room the entire time. Maybe she knew something.

She approached Coral, who spotted her coming and turned her back fully.

Beth supposed that was fair. Coral had a right to be angry with her. When Edward told her about his infidelity, she jumped to the obvious conclusion. Her mouth ran as it often did. But if not Abigail, then someone else had slept with her husband.

And she hated herself for thinking it, but the way Edward hovered over Destiny, his interest was a possessive one. He would always run from the house if Destiny needed him. She thought nothing of it until tonight. But the frail, gentle damsel would've been so enticing for Edward.

"I'm sorry," Beth whispered. "If tonight has taught me anything, it's that Abigail has no interest in an old beast like my husband."

"I worried it was true, to be honest," Coral said. "I've resented her for years over something she didn't do. I'm a terrible mother." Coral clapped her hand over her mouth to stop from crying.

Beth shook her head. "No, this is my fault. I should know to keep my mouth shut. I just can't help it sometimes. Where is your daughter now?"

"I don't know, I haven't seen her in some time. Joseph finally woke, though I think he wishes he hadn't. I just wish I knew how Carl was."

"I got an idea," Beth said, eyeing the sleepy boy. "Poor Joe isn't needed here. Send him to find his father and tell him the good news. Have him report back here when he's done."

Joseph, who was now aware of both women staring at him, only blinked.

"That is a good idea."

Beth left Coral to it and rejoined Sophie. "Any idea what happened?"

Sophie pursed her lips. Whatever she thought, her twin didn't want to say it.

"Oh, come on, this is important," Beth said.

Destiny's eyes were closed, and she emitted a soft purr. Sophie couldn't ignore her any longer.

Sophie stood and edged close to her. "Edward says she suffered exposure but can't figure out how. She's also intoxicated, but it's Edward doesn't think it to be alcohol."

Beth felt her insides twist. The disappearance and reappearance of her distilling set. It had been gone for weeks before reappearing in the same place she left it. Beth only told Edward of it, but if someone had made bad moonshine... But Destiny would have tasted it.

Naturally, Edward blamed Drew. He said that their son was probably making moonshine in the woods. "I did something similar as a boy his age."

Beth would have been inclined to agree with him, but what she did not tell her husband was that half of her poppy seeds went missing along with it. Drew wouldn't know how to make opium. He never observed her processes, and he was never the bookish type.

Only a learned person would know how to make opium. Someone with experience and a knack for distillation.

She wanted to relay the concerns to her husband. That someone had broken into her laboratory and took her still and poppy seeds and gave the resulting efforts to poor Destiny, but when Beth opened her mouth, pain quaked her mind.

Beth's vision went from black to red. Agony brought her to her knees. It was as if her jaw had dislocated and relocated all at once. Too brief and sharp to comprehend, it was all she could do to keep from crying out.

"Beth?" Sophie asked in alarm. "Are you okay?"

Just like that, it was gone.

An uncertain terror overcame her. What happened, and would it happen again? Beth didn't want to risk opening her mouth again. She gave her sister a nod and pretended that she was checking on Destiny. If Sophie suspected anything out of the ordinary, her sister let it go.

Helicant

One bottle was opened, and Helicant was uncorking another. The basement was somewhere she seldom went. No one other than her went down there at all. It was a dirt floor that had been pounded into a smooth finish over time. The wooden steps groaned with every step. The smell of damp dirt filled the air.

Most poignant was the small door in the basement. It was a thick pine with a heavy brass handle. There was a lock on it, but it had been left unhinged because Helicant's grandmother lost the key decades ago. It could only be opened from the outside anyways.

When she was a child, her grandfather took her down to the basement and showed her. While most thought their grandfather a bit of a kook, Helicant took a liking to him. He often showed the children the secrets of the island. But even the basement was considered off-limits, even for him.

If Grandfather dared not go, it must've been truly bad.

One evening, when grandmother was already in bed, Helicant's grandfather approached her. "You're going to inherit Sallows Hall; it's only fair you see what's inside."

She was afraid of what lurked in the basement. On the island of monsters, it was more than fair to imagine the worst. Helicant could still remember how she shivered as the earth floor leached the heat from her feet.

"Does grandma know what we are doing?"

"She does," her grandfather replied as he walked down the basement steps. "It was her idea."

Helicant swallowed hard and clamped her hands together. This wasn't one of Grandpa's funny games. It was a rite of passage. Her legacy. Helicant took in the earthen scent. Her grandfather's back remained to her until he reached the door.

"You see how it's sort of bricked in around the edges?" he said, pointing at the frame.

She did notice.

The door was framed by limestone bricks, and they overlapped several inches of the door itself, making it impossible to push open from the other side. The lock itself dangled from its handle uselessly.

Helicant's grandfather opened the door, and a gust of heat blew her hair back. Her grandfather handed her the lantern. "Step in, but don't stray from the door."

Despite the need to obey her elders, Helicant's feet were frozen in place. Between the conflicting orders to never go through the door and her grandfather's instructions was a reservoir of fears and anxiety of the unknown, and all of them lived and breathed on the other side of that door.

"I'm just going to show you how it works."

She took the lantern and stepped over the threshold. The lantern didn't provide enough light to show Helicant anything useful. It was warmer, but the floor felt no different on her feet than the floor in the basement. She couldn't see much else.

"I'm going to close it now," her grandfather said, pulling out his pocket watch. "It's eleven forty-six. I will open it at eleven forty-seven."

Helicant gave a nod, and the door closed.

On the other side, there was no handle. Once shut, there was no way to open it. Helicant's trembly hands felt along the seamless line where the door and limestone met. Even with the lock broken, nothing could get out.

Being the obedient child, she waited for her grandfather to open the door. It had been well past a minute. He was a silly old man. Perhaps he'd forgotten her. She knocked on the door. "Grandpa," she called.

She knew time was a tricky thing. When she was playing games and enjoying herself, it seemed to rush by. During lessons, time managed to draw on as if it were mocking her. Helicant didn't know much about science, but she understood there was a perfectly reasonable explanation for it.

Growing impatient, Helicant pounded on the door with her fist. "Open this door now!"

The darkness that surrounded her began to creep in. Helicant spun around, holding out her lantern as if it were a weapon. There was nothing there. Only the echo of drips in the distance. Helicant took a few steps forward and gasped as she realized she stood at a stairway.

Her mind began to map out just where she was standing.

Helicant stood squarely underneath Sallows Hall. She went left a few yards until she found that it was shaped like an L. This was the east wing. Returning to the door once more, Helicant took a deep breath and did the same for the right. Just as she thought. It was a replica of the west wing.

The catacombs were an extension of the home itself. Sallows Hall had four more levels and countless more rooms, only these rooms were without doors, furniture, or anything resembling a home. It was a dungeon without bars, allowing its inmates to travel freely within its tomb.

She had been there for far longer than a minute—Helicant knew this for certain. Though the monsters were said to be long gone, those pitch-black rooms without doors terrified her. She kept imagining that something would come shuffling out to get her. Helicant pounded on the door and cursed her grandfather.

Sobs burst from her proud little face as she fell to her knees, begging and pleading for someone to open the door. Helicant leaned against the wall beside the door so as to not obstruct anyone from opening it and cried. Her fingers traced what looked to be fingernail marks on the door from whatever poor soul was last trapped here.

Why would her grandfather do this to her? He loved her. Grandmother was a strict woman, but she was not unnecessarily cruel. Even if she did order this, grandfather wouldn't stand for it. Maybe he had no choice. Helicant fell in and out of sleep, her eyes sore from the diminishing light and the tears.

The lantern was nearly out of oil. A new fear rose in Helicant's throat. She couldn't be left there in the dark. Did her grandparents wish to kill her? Why would they do such a thing? Helicant let out a wail and clawed at the door until her fingers bled.

Suddenly, the door opened. Light flooded her eyes, and she had to squint. Helicant dove for the opening, knocking down her savior in the process. She shook all over and cried without tears. Helicant gasped and heaved until she nearly fainted.

"It's all right now."

Once she had recovered, Helicant slapped her beloved grandfather across the face. "How could you leave me!" she shouted.

Her grandfather pulled out his watch and tried to show her, but Helicant didn't care what time it was. She slapped the watch out of his hand, no longer caring if she was a good, obedient child. If they wanted her to be a lady, they should have treated her more fairly.

"Oh," her grandfather laughed. "It seems you've got your mother's spirit after all."

The basement door was closed, and grandfather was still reaching for his watch now on the ground. He opened it up and gave it to her. "Look," he said.

Helicant only glared at him in the low lantern light.

"Look!"

She looked. It was eleven forty-seven. There was no way that could be accurate, but Grandfather's watch was never late. He wound it each morning before breakfast. He showed her the time before she stepped into the catacombs for a reason. This was what her grandparents needed her to know as heir to Sallows Hall.

Helicant never spoke of what happened to anyone.

Now that Destiny was to be the head of the family, she would have no choice but to show her. The very idea of subjecting Destiny to such cruelty was unfathomable. Still, it was something Destiny would need to learn, and Helicant was running out of time.

She shook the gruesome memories from her mind. There was far too much going on tonight to dwell on the past. And whatever came next, Helicant was certain that Daniel could help her daughter.

His proposal may have been the sincerest words ever uttered in the mansion. Even she would have difficulty declining a man who made such a passionate speech.

Yet, for all his warmth, Daniel had also been calculating.

Daniel was vowing to grow with Destiny, to work with her to make themselves something better. It was what marriage should be. He was romantic at heart, no doubt. Still, even in Destiny's panicked state, she understood just how special it was to have a partner like that in life.

William was practical.

He had oatmeal and eggs every morning and read a half hour before bed each night. Nothing changed in him, and Helicant appreciated that, but deep down, she found herself craving more.

Edward was overcome by his desire for her. It was a contagious sort of romance. It boiled over and ruined everything but evaporated just as soon as it arrived, sparing nothing in its wake. If William knew about them, he never gave it away. If he even cared.

The cork finally came dislodged from the wine bottle, but once freed, the curve of the bottle collapsed in on itself, and Helicant found herself holding a handful of tinted glass. The bottle fell to the floor, and the red wine pooled around her feet. There was a sting in her palm as she released her grip. Most of the glass fragments fell to the floor. Some remained embedded in her skin.

Helicant let out a cry of shock. Her hands trembled as she tried to pull shards out of her palm. Doing so created more of a mess. Blood spouted from deep cuts through several layers of skin, and she was starting to feel faint. Staggering away from the wreckage, Helicant found herself slumping against the door to the catacombs.

She was unable to process what was happening, but she might've been dying.

The metallic smell overwhelmed her. Helicant's neck grew weak, and her head lolled back as she inhaled the sweet perfume. Clutching her wounded palm, warm blood flowed and dried on her thin skin.

Helicant released the pressure on her wounds for a moment, only to feel faint again at the sight.

It wasn't just the injury or the blood loss that rendered Helicant helpless. It was the belly aching hunger. She had always been anemic. Her body was crying out for the loss of something it desperately needed.

"I'm to return again? So soon?"

It was almost carnal in its need. Drips of blood fell to the earthen floor, and Helicant swallowed hard and resisted the urge to not lick the ground.

In the end, she gave in to her desires as she always did. She let go of her hand, exposing the wound to the sting of air before latching on with her mouth. Blood and fragments of glass came spilling into her mouth. She devoured it all without hesitation. She felt release when she drank.

She let out a moan of ecstasy as she felt life returning to her once more, and when the bleeding slowed, she bit into her torn flesh. Helicant ignored the dull pain of teeth gnashing into skin and bit deeper into the tender, fatty flesh underneath. She couldn't deny the irresistible chew. It itched a scratch she had felt her entire life.

In those fleeting moments, a truth surfaced from deep in her heart. She no longer cared about decency or ceremony. She was not the matron of some important family. She was the descendant of a royal bastard who took on an impossible task to claim prominence denied to them.

She wasn't a mother, a widow, and a sister.

Helicant was a monster.

Abigail

When Destiny fainted, it was like watching a beloved idol fall. Destiny's nearly pulled her to the ground. Nobody made a move to help her. It was all about her cousin. She supposed it was only fair since Destiny was the new matron, but Abigail didn't enjoy being shoved out of the way like an old carpet bag.

Helicant was quicker than any old woman should be.

She had a hold of Destiny's arm but was unable to pull her daughter up due to the dead weight. Daniel was the closest and on his feet, ready to catch her. Shouts of alarm sounded throughout the room.

"Let me have a look," Edward said, shoving past Abigail in his zeal to get to Destiny.

"Don't you touch her," Helicant hissed.

Edward looked most indignant. "I'm her doctor!"

Abigail took several steps back. Her mentor said doctor, but it felt as though he wanted to say something else. As if he had a claim to Destiny that could dispute Daniel's? He had always seen to her cousin personally, driving a wedge between them. For the first time, Abigail couldn't help but suspect there was a reason other than doctoring.

Drew's eyes flickered with recognition. What did he know? She spent more time with worn, outdated physician books than she did with the people on this island.

"And she's my wife," Daniel said.

Daniel was not backing down, not even to her doctor. It was shocking, really. Abigail had never seen him so fierce... So possessive. Even Helicant hesitated.

"Both of you, come with me," Daniel said as he strode out of the room, Destiny in his arms. Helicant and Edward followed behind as though he were the one in charge. Abigail had never seen her brother so commanding and confident. She nearly let out a cheer. Maybe all Daniel ever needed was something to fight for.

Abigail slunk out the door with the three of them and closed the drawing room door behind her.

"We should bring her to the downstairs bathroom," Helicant said. "It has a sofa she can rest on. The one on this level is more of a facilities room."

Only, when they descended the stairs, Abigail didn't follow. When no one was paying attention, Abigail creeped up the stairs, occasionally checking to make sure no one noticed. Abigail went up to the fourth floor. She snuck into Helicant's room, went to her nightstand drawer, and pulled out a leather case holding several syringes, a tie, and a small bottle of opium.

She thought about injecting then and there, but Abigail didn't want to risk being found all strung out in Helicant's room. She decided the best thing to do would be to use one of the abandoned rooms. Slipping out the door, Abigail selected an empty room at random. It was four doors down and around the corner.

The room was plain. There were no linens or curtains in the room. There was a bedroom set in this one, though it too was simple and made of pine. Abigail took a seat before setting up the syringe.

Edward made her practice on herself with a syringe many times. She could find a vein; she could make it hurt or not. All injections were given to her to administer, but seldom did anyone need it. The only exception was Helicant needing opium on occasion for debilitating migraines or if Abigail's father hurt his back.

She welcomed the needle's bite as it punctured her skin. The opium crawled through her veins and brought their pathetic existence to a standstill. A rush of warmth and euphoria welcomed her, beckoned her to set sail.

Floating in and out of consciences. Half-dreaming, she explored parts of the island unknown to anyone else. Slipping into a lucid state where she saw the monsters her family told her didn't exist.

Drew was there as well. Only he was afraid and humbled—that she knew to be a dream. Edward's face when his eyes scanned up and down her body in the black slinky dress as if he were seeing her for the first time. Sophie's arms bent in the wrong direction. Daniel's relief when Destiny said yes. A hideous creature with horns and claws chasing Beth. Her mother playing with her sewing kit in her pocket. A rabbit with horns and fangs. Abigail's children, their numbers countless and hungry. Awaiting their feast.

When she awoke, Abigail slinked from the room and returned the case from where she found it.

The stairway was oddly quiet. She pressed her ear against the drawing room and heard voices. Destiny wasn't speaking, but people were speaking to her, so it seemed she had recovered from her fainting spell.

Helicant would blame Abigail. The corset was small, but she didn't tighten it nearly as much as she could've. Destiny wasn't corset trained the way the old women were; she couldn't handle that, not on this day.

Sophie had yet to return to the kitchen, and Beth hadn't taken up where her twin left off. It was strange since it was well past dinner, and all the food was left out. Not wanting it to get too cold, she put them back on the stovetop to warm. She noticed the back door was open, too.

Knowing full well that Helicant wasn't a fan of open doors in the fall, Abigail moved to shut the door, but as she did, she saw Drew standing in the yard, his face awash with conflict or self-pity. He stood there all alone as the fog rolled in. His figure was outlined in the moonlight over the hedge maze.

She didn't care if he was alone or sad, Abigail told herself as much, but it didn't stop her from going out to meet him. The wind blew and chilled her, forcing Abigail to wrap her arms around herself tightly.

"It's a bit cold for brooding," she teased.

He did a double take as if he didn't recognize her for a moment, but as he stepped toward her, Drew removed his jacket and put it around her shoulders. "I just need a break."

"I did, too."

Despite her past notions of Drew, Abigail found herself feeling a different way about him on this day. Perhaps it was all the conversation about marriage, but he seemed more interested in talking to her than pushing her in the mud or making a snide remark like he did when they were younger.

"Come," she said. "Let's walk around the manor together."

Drew shook his head. "I'm afraid everyone will be quite cross with me."

She thought about the corset and said, "They're probably angry with me too. Come on. The house is so big, no one will find us unless we want them to."

"You don't understand," Drew said with his head bowed. "I gave Destiny a scare. I wasn't going to hurt her—I just wanted to piss off my father."

Normally, she'd find this childish, but the way Edward cast her aside for Destiny had stirred complicated feelings for her. It made sense logically; Destiny was fainting, and he was her doctor. It cut her deeper than she wanted to admit. Not once had Edward looked at her with such fear in his eyes. Abigail was his protégé, his mentee. He spent more time with her than he did with his own wife, and yet...

"We both have been holding our breath, waiting for Edward to give us what we need. I think we should stop waiting for him," she took his hand in her own and pulled Drew into the house.

Together, she and Drew snuck into the back alley that stretched past the old laundry room. Abigail peeked around the corner to make sure no one was coming before she gave Drew a nod, and they made a run for the stairs. She heard Edward's voice but couldn't make out what he was saying. No one else seemed to be talking.

Drew was eager to get away from the drawing room and in the open, where they could be seen, so Abigail didn't get a chance to hear anything else. There were no signs of life on the third story. "The west wing is entirely closed on this level," Abigail explained. "Destiny is afraid of getting lost."

"I thought she was afraid of green eyes," Drew mused.

"She is, but that's only part of it."

The side of Drew's mouth scrunched up as if he wanted to smile but didn't get the joke.

"We read Nathaniel's diary as children," Abigail explained. "In the diary, they talk of a green-eyed monster that they couldn't lock in the catacombs beneath the manor and imprisoned it somewhere in the house itself."

"Oh," Drew said. "She's afraid of accidentally encountering the room with the monster with green eyes. That would make for a horrid nightmare."

"That's not the creepy part."

Drew raised his brows.

"She had the nightmare before we read the book."

Abigail didn't want to continue the conversation. It gave her goose-bumps just thinking about it. She remembered the night Destiny woke up screaming and clawing at her blankets, rendered speechless by the nightmare, the smell of urine ripe in the air. Helicant came in running. She held Destiny despite fingernails scratching at her face and arms.

She wasn't invited to sleepovers after that. Abigail told Destiny that it was okay, that she wasn't afraid of her cousin's night terrors, but she never stayed the night again. Destiny became more reclusive and hidden—like a wounded animal crouching in the dark. Their close friendship became more like an acquaintance after that. Abigail always thought it was Destiny's anxiety that was the source of their separation, but after seeing the way Edward reacted, she wasn't so certain.

Drew led her up to the fourth flight of steps. "Oh, the east wing is partially open up here."

Abigail showed Drew the other half of the mansion. She remembered that a few rooms were fully furnished from helping Helicant with some spring cleaning. Though she couldn't quite remember which room was which.

Drew shook his head. "I'm not even sure where I am anymore."

"It's fun, isn't it?"

"I feel like we need a trail of breadcrumbs or some string."

"Destiny tried both—Helicant nearly tripped and fell down the stairs on the string. She took to creating little dolls and hanging them on rooms she knows to be safe."

Abigail opened one of the doors on the left side and revealed a room similar in size to Helicant's room. It was a bedroom that extended into a small living room and was set up with a washroom, but the plumbing had been removed. An old bowl and basin replaced what was once a fully functioning lavatory.

There were white linens on the four-poster bed and some pale-yellow curtains that somewhat clashed against the green with red floral wallpaper. She closed the door behind them as Drew went to have a look out the window.

"This room isn't in the blueprint." Drew scanned the room with a laugh.

"I know. I've brought it up before. It seems the previous owners did some renovations after the map was made."

Drew's pale face was glowing from the light. His hair looked redder, but his freckles less prominent. Still, he was strikingly handsome. In the moonlight, he looked more like Edward somehow. Abigail approached him and traced along his jawline. Brown eyes gazed into hers curiously.

"I thought you and my father…"

Abigail shook her head. "No, it seems he prefers blondes."

"You noticed that too?"

"He always had a noted interest in her, but whenever he did house calls, I would be sent to do something else."

"Helicant hates him," Drew added. "If I were a mother of such a fragile girl, I'd hate her much older lover too."

Abigail cringed and tried to push it out of her mind and focus on Drew instead. Edward would regret ignoring her just as her mother did. Her mother wanted her to marry Drew, not sleep with him, but she never could do just what her mother wanted.

She kissed him then, nearly on the tips of her toes just to reach his lips. Drew responded by pulling her in at the waist. His hands raked across the smooth fabric of her dress as he explored the curves of her back. He pulled away, gasping for air as if praying for restraint.

"Don't hold back," she told him.

Beth

Destiny was coming around, and her head no longer wobbled on her neck like a newborn baby. Her eyes were growing clearer as she became more aware of her surroundings. Daniel and Edward were on either side of the bride. Beth noted some rather terse expressions between them, but she chalked it up to worry.

Coral fretted over Carl, the poor silly thing. Joseph had left some time ago, but he'd yet to return with any news.

"How are you feeling, dear?" Sophie asked.

"Better," Destiny said without making eye contact.

"Where's my mother?" Destiny asked.

Oh. Beth should know the answer to such a simple question. She looked to Sophie, who gave a shrug. Her twin had no idea either. "I haven't seen her since Daniel brought Destiny into the house."

"Beth," Edward said. "Be a dear and see if you can't find her? She will be most cross if we don't let her know what's going on."

"It's not like we know ourselves," Beth said. Gods only knew where her sister was; it was better to wait for her to return. Besides, she wanted to know what happened to Destiny. The girl remained silent, but her hands were wrung like she was about to tell everyone what the fuss was about.

"Beth, please," Sophie said. "She needs her mother."

Slamming the sliding door shut, Beth went to fetch Helicant. She wasn't a complete moron. Whatever happened, Destiny didn't want to say in front of her. Beth had been cast off enough times that she knew when she wasn't wanted.

Though she would find out one way or another.

Where would she even begin to search for Helicant? She had half a mind to call out for her sister if it weren't so impolite. The last place she was supposed to be was the basement getting wine. It wouldn't have taken her sister that long, so perhaps Helicant was preparing the dining room. With all of Destiny's damsel theatrics, dinner had run rather late.

The stained-glass double doors depicted the fox on the hillside, outrunning the hunters. Sophie said it was an allegory for religious persecution. When the Christians took over Pagan nations, they hunted those who never did conform. The clever fox could always hide in the forest and in its burrows, whereas the hunters trespassed on lands that didn't belong to them.

Turning the worn brass knobs, Beth opened both doors wide to find the room was still dimly lit. The long wooden table was accompanied by mostly matching chairs (save for two slightly newer versions that didn't match exactly). The tablecloth was laid, and so were the placemats and most of the plates.

None of the silverware, goblets, or napkins were laid out. Nor were the good candles to properly illuminate the room. The centerpieces were red roses and an assortment of wildflowers that remained despite the turn of the season. The wild roses must've been parched, the vase was nearly empty, so before she left, Beth used the pitcher on the table to refill it. She hoped Helicant wouldn't notice the few splashes of water on the tablecloth.

The kitchen was also empty.

Dishes of food were moved to the stovetop to keep warm, but the fire burned low. She shook her head and tossed a few small chunks of wood into the oven, then dusted off her hands. It would suffice for now, just until everyone was rounded up for dinner.

The sky was dark now. It was drawing later in the evening, nearly eight o'clock by her estimate. Helicant would be cross with how late dinner was, but what else could they do? Considering that Destiny said yes to Daniel, the outcome was still a happy one.

"Helicant?" Beth called.

If her sister wasn't here, perhaps she would be in her bedroom? Beth couldn't see why Helicant would go there unless she had taken ill.

There was a shrill groan from the basement. Her belly sank at the sound. Helicant. She was an old woman... She must have fallen. Beth rushed down the stairs. Helicant wouldn't stay down there a moment longer than necessary. Everyone feared the basement, even the matron. Especially the matron.

She could smell the blood halfway down the stairs. A tacky, iron tang assaulted her sinuses and lingered in the back of her throat. She needed to grip the railings as her knees were not what they used to be. "Helicant?"

There was no reply. Beth swore she heard what sounded like chewing and slurping. "What on earth is going on here?"

Beth moved toward the lantern. She stepped into a puddle of something but ignored it. Turning up the lantern light, Beth turned to find Helicant on the ground up against the catacomb door. Her sister had blood smeared along her mouth, and she was gnawing fiercely on her own hand with a vacant look in her eyes.

"Helicant," Beth gasped. "What's happened to you?"

Her sister's facial features protruded sharply, exaggerated by the shadows, giving her a younger, though demonic visage. Whatever creature her sister was in that moment, it did not recognize her. It moved into a defensive position on palms and haunches before letting out a deafening scream.

Beth, too, tried to scream.

Only when she did, her jaw spasmed wildly as though her tongue had become dislocated from her throat. She gagged and fell to her knees in the muck and glass left on the floor. Something was happening to her that she didn't understand.

In her last fleeting moments, Beth thought she heard her husband's voice. She reached out for him in silence. Edward wasn't as strong as he pretended. She worried he wouldn't be okay. The pain rang between her ears and stopped her breathing. Drew would be okay. Beth clutched her chest. The last thing she saw was the stained earth floor.

Destiny

No one said anything when Beth left the room. Nor did anyone speak when Edward reached into the secret book to take out the whiskey. He poured himself and Daniel a cup before approaching Destiny. He pinched his trousers and pulled them up before he sat in her mother's chair. Sophie, every faithful Sophie, still sat by her side.

"Did Drew threaten you?" He asked.

Destiny nodded. "He tried to rape me."

Daniel was standing directly behind her, so while she couldn't see his reaction, Edward shot him a warning glance and motioned for him to wait. Coral gasped and shook her head, and Destiny heard the decanter uncorked. Sophie didn't bother with a glass.

"Are you certain he wasn't joking?" Coral asked. "He's crude, but—"

"How could you even think that?" Sophie asked.

"I just want to remove any doubt."

"The only doubt to be had is whether or not your daughter can still marry the bastard," Sophie raged.

Coral's voice went high as she tried to argue it further but was cut off by Daniel. "If Destiny says it was his intent, it was his intent."

His voice carried a sharper, almost more dangerous edge that felt like a dagger's point dragged along glass. So much was at stake. The consequences would reverberate throughout the island. She couldn't look Edward in the eyes. Drew had never done anything to hurt her before. He was her cousin, a playmate as a child. He was to be Abigail's partner. Edward and Beth's only son.

"I'm sorry," she said, her lips trembling.

Destiny felt arms around her shoulders, and she eased into Daniel. "You have no reason to be sorry."

"Indeed not." Edward agreed, "You're very brave."

"Can you tell us more about what happened?" Daniel asked.

Destiny wiped her eyes and smiled. His presence was reassuring despite the danger. Tilting her head up, she just wanted a glance at his face. She didn't know why. Her vision blurred, and the slightest hint of his eyes was enough to set her off. Her chest seized instantly, and she began hyperventilating.

Daniel clasped his eyes shut. "Now why would you go and do a thing like that?"

Edward grabbed her hand, gave it a steady shake, and chuckled. "You outwitted a skilled hunter, and now you're looking the devil in the eye."

"I...I just wanted to see you," she told him. "I thought it would make me feel better."

"Didn't work, did it?" Daniel laughed.

Destiny wasn't so sure.

She turned to Edward and said, "Drew put something in my drink to slow me down. He also thinks you and I are..."

It took Edward a minute to realize what Destiny was trying to imply. "Oh," he said before standing. "It would seem this was partly my fault then."

He approached the fireplace mantle and took a sip of his drink. "Earlier today, I told him to stay away from you. I think he took it as a sort of challenge."

Sophie shook her head. "That in no way condones what he tried to do."

"There's more," Destiny said.

Edward wouldn't look at her. He focused on his drink. Rotated it in his palm watching the crystal reflect the light. "Several months back, I wanted to do some solo hunting. I nearly fell into a trap. I knew it was one of Drew's. That trap led to another trap and then another. It wasn't long before I came upon a camouflaged cave."

"What was in it?" Destiny asked.

Edward looked up at the beast carved into the mantle. "Various animal parts in different stages of decomposition. Some looked like they had been there for a while. Others were... Fresh. Many were dissected. I suspect they were alive when he did his experiments."

"I'm going to find Carl," Coral said as she fled the room.

Destiny didn't blame her. She felt as though she were going to be sick again. She found herself hanging on to Daniel's arm. "Edward..."

She felt so sorry for him. Edward had been keeping this secret all this time. That was why he told Drew to leave her alone. Why he so readily believed that Drew attacked her. Her mother had to have known on some level what Drew was. Destiny doubted her mother would overlook Drew for her engagement just because Abigail would be alone otherwise.

"This is my responsibility," Edward said. "He will never hurt anyone again."

"What do you mean to do?" Daniel asked.

Edward looked at them. "What I must."

There was a yell coming from outside the drawing room. Everyone turned to look at the door, but of course, there was nothing to see.

"You think it's Beth?" Sophie asked.

Edward rolled his eyes. "She probably saw a spider. They always come out in the fall time."

Sophie opened the door and looked out on the steps, but there was no further noise. She turned back to face them and shrugged. "It was probably a spider."

Edward nodded grimly. "Do me a favor and keep this quiet. I will deal with Beth when it's time, but first, we just need to get through this night."

"Where do you think he is now?" Destiny asked.

"I don't imagine he will show his face again. Not tonight at least."

"I won't let you leave my sight," Daniel vowed.

Destiny appreciated the sentiment, but she wasn't afraid as much as she was angry and disgusted. Drew tried to rape her to make a point to his father that he was the one who controlled this island. Except that neither of them was the head of the family. She was.

"You can keep it from Beth all you like," Destiny said, standing on wobbly legs. "But you are not the leader of this island. You don't get to decide what happens to him; my mother does."

Edward's brows raised in surprise. "That is somewhat true. However, the official leader of the island wears that ring," he said, pointing at the ring on her hand.

Right. She was now the matron. It didn't change her, but there was a bout of self-confidence that wasn't there before. She was the one to bestow judgment, not her mother. This would be a mercy for Drew.

She didn't want to even consider what sort of punishment her mother would've bestowed.

"Daniel and I will go to Sophie's cottage," Destiny said. "She had an old pair of flintlocks we can use as protection. Drew won't look for us there."

"We can hear gunshots from nearly any point on the island," she told Edward. "If you encounter any trouble, we will likely hear you. Bring Drew back to the house. We will decide what to do with him then."

"I should stay here in case anyone comes back," Sophie said.

"What if Drew comes after you?"

"What would Drew want with an old bird like me?" Sophie asked. "Besides, Beth and Helicant are still around here somewhere."

Destiny supposed that was true. Someone would need to reel those two in. There was still the matter of telling Beth. She decided that it didn't matter how Beth learned that her son was a psychotic torturer and attempted rapist. What mattered was protecting everyone else on the island.

She took a hold of Daniel's hand, more reserved with her gaze. "Shall we go then?"

Daniel gave her hand a little squeeze and... For a moment, she was nostalgic. Transported to a time when her father walked about the house with her, holding her hand so she wouldn't get lost. Yes, Daniel's eyes were terrifying, but in the dream, she was always alone. With him by her side, her night terror couldn't actualize.

They left through the servant's exit. Daniel checked for signs of Drew. Destiny wished Drew would show his face. Drew was nearly a foot taller and at least three-stone heavier than her. If he needed to resort to drugging her, he was no match for her sober.

The evening fog rolled along valleys along the island, making Sallows Hall feel as though it were a much smaller island in the clouds. The crescent moon dipped below the treetops but was bright enough to light the way to Sophie's cottage.

Destiny took a chance and looked at Daniel's face. His cheeks were a tad round, but he was a fine-looking man. She was glad that he took after his mother because Daniel looked nothing like Abigail or Joseph. His eyes still frightened her, but his mindfulness of her condition only spurred her confidence. It wasn't just a silly fear to him; it mattered. He understood her pain and didn't dismiss it. She didn't think it possible, and yet...

"I still can't believe it," Daniel said.

"That we're married?"

"Well, yes, of course."

Daniel wasn't referring to their marriage. A lot happened on this day, and his concerns were the more immediate ones. "You mean Drew."

"I suppose the day in general," he said. "When I woke up this morning, I was convinced you'd say no. Everyone was. Then Drew had to go and lose his mind. So, here we are, spending our honeymoon on a manhunt."

It wasn't how she imagined the day turning out either. Absently, she spun the ring on her finger. "I was under the impression that only the doctor knew how bad it was."

"We heard rumors, but that wasn't why I thought you'd say no."

If not a crippling phobia, why else would she say no? He was implying his deficiency was obvious, but it wasn't to her. Destiny hugged herself for warmth. She didn't like feeling so naive. "Why would I say no if not for the eyes?"

"Well," Daniel's voice clipped with uncertainty. "I'm not as handsome as Drew or Joseph."

His weight. It must've been a sensitive issue for him, but to her, it was nonsense. Drew tortured and dismembered animals and tried to rape her. Those weren't handsome qualities. And to her, Daniel was far more attractive than Joseph.

"I don't like Drew or Joseph," she said. "I wouldn't marry either, even if Mother ordered me to."

"So you said yes to the guy you can barely face?"

"I was going to say no," Destiny admitted. "But when you proposed, I forgot how scared I was."

Destiny let go of his hand and walked in front of him to face Daniel.

In the darkness, she could see the hint of his green eyes glaring back at her. Her heart pounded, and she swallowed with fear but shook her head, refusing to bow down to it.

"I'm done being afraid," she told him. "I know it won't go away overnight and that sometimes it will be too hard to handle, but I refuse to let it get in the way anymore."

Daniel's face was unreadable in that moment. He could see her shaking hands and looked down to give her a moment's reprieve before saying, "You haven't changed after all."

She didn't know what he meant. Changed from what?

He caught up with her, taking her hand, and they resumed walking. "Do you remember the time Drew put a frog down Abigail's dress?"

Destiny remembered all at once and started laughing loudly. Her cackle carried into the still night. Daniel laughed quietly. "It seems you do."

"I forgot all about it."

"You lunged out of nowhere and bit him!"

Destiny laughed so hard she was crying. She must've been five or six. How did she let such memories slip away? That was the true curse of mental illness. It whittled away at her self-esteem and faded otherwise bright memories.

"Serves him right," Daniel said. "I'll never forget Helicant chasing you around the yard with a switch. The scariest woman I've ever met, and you told her you were going to bite her too."

Destiny cringed. Yes, she was wild. Poor mother, it was all she could do to keep up with a small, feral little girl in a big house. "Oh, she wasn't that mad. You just don't know her like I do."

Daniel cast her a side glance as a rebuttal. He actually didn't believe her. If she didn't know better, she'd think he was afraid of an old lady.

"My mother seems harsh, but she's quite a pushover. If she knows it's important to you, she will forgive most things. She's fiercely protective, though."

"I bet."

"She once filed my fingernails for an entire month because I scratched myself in my sleep."

"How old were you?"

"I was seventeen," Destiny stared up at the sky and sighed. "I had a night terror and scratched myself on accident. She said I didn't file my nails properly."

"I imagine between the night terrors and that fever... Edward asked my dad to build a small casket, you know."

Destiny's heart stopped for a moment. Not because Edward thought she was so close to death as a child, but because she knew how hard her mother would have taken it.

"Mother never saw it, right?"

"No," Daniel shook his head. "I don't think he made it. It was shortly after that you started having the night terrors. I wonder if that has something to do with it."

Destiny shrugged. There could have been a correlation between the night terrors and the fever, but knowing why it started didn't really change anything for her now. What mattered now was getting over it. Allowing that part of her to grow a thick skin so that one day, she could look Daniel in the eyes and not come undone.

The hedges that separated the cottage grounds from the mansion were in sight. "There it is!"

"Um, Destiny?" Daniel paused.

"Hm?" She tried to look again but looked away from his eyes at the last second.

"Are we allowed to be alone together?"

They were married, weren't they? Mother said that it would be up to them to decide on personal matters. There was emphasis on needing a partner, and what came after that was entirely up to her, but maybe Coral had different rules.

"Your mother had a lot of expectations, didn't she?"

Daniel shrugged. "With me not so much. I just remember how upset she was when Abigail became Edward's apprentice. It meant they would be together alone. I don't want your mother upset with us like that."

"I know the ceremony didn't happen, but the marriage is legal. Mother made it so. Besides, you're married to the matron now, and we don't have to answer to anyone anymore."

It was too dark to see his face, but something in his stride was more confident. She didn't tell him that she needed to remind herself of that fact every few minutes or that she herself wanted nothing more than to cling to her mother's skirts. Destiny would have to pretend until it felt real.

They were just about to enter the cottage when something rustled in the bushes nearby. Daniel grasped Destiny in fear as Destiny squinted to see further. "It's probably an animal."

"We should get you inside," he said with no small amount of urgency.

"Hey!" She shouted and picked up a rock. Destiny threw the rock at the bush, and something cried and jumped straight off the cliff.

It didn't look like any animal she had ever seen. Squat with leathery wings, she moved closer towards the bush when a pair of arms wrapped around her waist. Daniel had had enough and was practically lifting her from around the waist as he pulled her into the cottage before shutting and barring the doors and windows.

Helicant

When Helicant regained consciousness, she found herself on the very fainting couch that she last saw Destiny on. As amusing as it was, this was unexpected. The day's events had gotten away from her. In a world of limited possibilities, Destiny had said yes, and this changed things beyond Helicant's well-charted territory.

A dull throb pierced through her palm every so often until she rolled her head to the left and saw why.

The cut ran deep along the lifeline of her palm. The edges of her thin skin created a rocky terrain along what might've been a clean cut otherwise. She remembered the wine. Remembered cutting her hand, but it was all a blur after that. Something thought to make a meal of her. Imagining a fat, dirty rat chewing on her palm made her shiver.

"Hold still," Edward ordered. "I've got my work cut out for me."

"Where is everyone?" She asked.

"No need to worry about that now."

He only said that because there was something to worry about. "Did she change her mind? Did everyone go home?"

Edward shook his head. "Daniel and Destiny are fine. They are off frolicking, getting acquainted."

And why was this such a problem? Did he not want Destiny to be happy? No, there was something else on his mind. The doctor's face was pale and gaunt. His eyes were a bloody shade as if he had scratched at them. "What happened, Edward?"

Thread pulled through her broken skin. He pulled it taut, but Helicant refused to flinch in his presence. "Where to start?"

As is in his nature, when Edward started, he couldn't stop. He told her about the state Daniel found Destiny in. About the nature of her intoxication and the dwindling heat of her skin. Had Daniel not found her daughter when he did, she might've died of exposure despite being outside for less than an hour.

Her brave girl had no idea what was happening to her. Helicant allowed herself to feel the rage. She imagined all the things she wanted to do to Drew. He'd suffer. Oh, she'd make him beg for death but leave it just out of reach. She knew just what to do.

"You're to castrate him, but make sure he recovers from the procedure. After that, he goes where all the monsters go."

She didn't know how long someone could survive in the cellar, but it would feel like an eternity, and that was good enough for her.

Edward shook his head.

Steam built in her chest. She jerked her hand away to make him look at her. "What do you mean, no? Don't tell me it's for Beth's sake."

"It has nothing to do with Beth," Edward explained. "You gave the ring to Destiny. She has already ordered me to find him and bring him to the mansion to await her orders."

Helicant was taken aback by the idea of Destiny telling anyone what to do. The needle pricked her skin, and she resisted the urge to lick the fresh blood off her palm.

"Destiny is just a girl; she doesn't know what's best. She will forgive us."

Mercy was a mistake children made. No doubt Destiny would be swayed by the mothers hoping for grandchildren, but a bad seed was a bad seed. Helicant had known about Drew's little cave of horrors. She should've put an end to him in the morning while everyone slept.

The tug on the thread had a feel of finality to it. Helicant looked to see a jagged line from her thumb all the way down the side of her wrist.

"What happened?" she said, marveling at the wound.

Edward stood beside the partially rotted changing curtain. "I was hoping you would know."

"I cut myself on a broken wine bottle. I don't remember anything after that."

Edward didn't say anything. He just stared at the moonlight.

"If Beth is what you're concerned about, you need not worry about her. Once Drew is dead, you can stay with us. With me."

After all, that was what he wanted. His reaction was lacking. Lips still thin and grim. "That is what you want, isn't it?"

"I once told you that I'd give anything to be with you. If you had accepted then, Drew would have never been born, and Beth would still be alive."

Helicant bolted upright. "What?"

"Beth is dead," Edward said. "I found her in the basement with you. Her lower jawbone dislocated. She probably died of shock from..." Edward choked as he tried to restrain his sobs.

"Who?" she whispered. "Where is she?"

Helicant stood clumsily and took two steps for the door before falling back on the couch. It didn't alter her course. Using her wounded hand, she left bloody stamps across the sofa as she moved towards the door.

Edward tilted his head and laughed. "Oh, Helicant. You need to rest. Her body isn't going anywhere for now."

"Show me," she said. "Bring me to her or I'll—"

Edward steered her from under the arms until she was too tired to resist and fell back on the sofa. "Or what? You'll bleed out all over the bathroom? Lie down."

With far more force than needed, Edward pushed Helicant onto the sofa by her shoulders. He was too close. She could smell the stench of whiskey. Even still, her eyes lingered on his lips. Why was she cursed with an attraction to a drunk?

"Who was last seen with her?"

"You, my dear."

Helicant would have spat on him if she weren't lying down. Instead, she slapped him across the face with her good hand. Edward's head jerked with the slap. He gritted his teeth, ignoring the pain. "You were the only one in the room with her."

"Unconscious," Helicant argued. Whatever he was insinuating, she didn't like it. Nothing would lead her to hurting the twins. They were like daughters to her.

"Not at first you weren't."

Helicant narrowed her eyes and relaxed, allowing Edward to let go of her. He resumed sitting on the stool and explained further. "Sophie and I went down to the basement, where we found Beth dead on the floor. Her jaw..."

She had to remind herself to breathe and release her bawled fist. After what Edward told her about Drew, there was no doubt in her mind that he was the one who murdered her sister—his own mother.

"Say it," she whispered, though she wanted him to stop more than anything.

"I've never seen anything like it. The jaw was torn away from the skull, but the muscles were still attached. The skin wasn't torn, merely stretched. It's horrid to look at. Like a mockery of my wife."

"And you…"

"And me," Helicant said.

"You were in the corner, hissing like a feral beast trapped in the corner. You were chewing on your hand. Blood was smeared all over your face. Poor Sophie, she didn't see you, I don't think. She was too distraught by the sight of Beth."

She didn't want to believe him, but Helicant knew it to be the truth. Edward never lied about the flaws and shortcomings of others, though he was quick to forget his own. He never missed an opportunity to tell her the truth about herself.

The metallic tang in her mouth sang sweetly between her teeth. No, he didn't lie.

Despite hearing her own bizarre behavior, Helicant couldn't will herself to care. Beth was dead. Yes, her sister was annoying and troublesome, but she was her sister nonetheless. Beth always wanted to match Sophie as a child. Peas were her favorite vegetable. She sang when she did chores. All these things that Beth would no longer do filled Helicant with grief and rage for the person who put an end to her life.

Helicant's heart was beating loudly between her ears. "Do you know where Drew is now?"

"I don't know if Drew could have done this," Edward said. "The skin and muscle, there's no way a person could be responsible."

What was he even suggesting? None of this made sense to Helicant, and the throbbing in her hand only made it harder to think. She tried to recall what happened in the basement, but her head grew cloudy, and visions she couldn't explain came to her mind.

Not of the basement but of other things.

This hadn't happened before, or at least if it did, she was always the first to go. Helicant should've gone first.

She was crying. Tears pooled into her neck, and she wiped the troublesome moisture away and sniffed back the rest. Crying wouldn't bring Beth back. The surface of her face felt notably different. The protrusions were more pronounced, and her once wrinkled and sagged skin felt taught.

"Edward?"

"Hm?"

"Could you bring me that hand mirror?"

Staring at the white-tiled ceiling, she could sense his hesitation. "Edward."

"I think you should rest."

Helicant resisted the urge to lash out at him. What Edward lacked in self-control manifested itself in controlling everything else. He was trying to protect her from something he couldn't explain. But she needed to see...

"You can't explain it. You can't explain any of this, but I still need to see it."

There was a long pause, followed by the sound of something being lifted from the vanity table. Helicant took the ornate hand mirror that was offered to her by a pair of rather hairy hands.

"I...I know. It's as though it happened overnight."

"Matches your claws."

Edward's hand jerked away in embarrassment. Helicant was on the verge of making a witty comment, but what she saw in the mirror stopped her dead. The subtle bone protrusions on her temples, jaw-line, chin, and nose were now even sharper and more pronounced.

They looked as though they would cut through her skin at any moment.

Not only that, but she was notably younger. The dark circles under Helicant's eyes had faded, and some of her skin's youthful resiliency had returned. She was still old and wrinkled, but she looked as though she had regained ten years—and that made an astonishing difference at her age.

Helicant touched them. Even though she understood the nature of the curse and its grip on the island, it never ceased to astonish.

"Helicant, what's happening to us?"

"I don't know."

This was a lie, but lying to Edward was nothing new. It didn't matter if she told him or not. If Destiny failed to break the curse, the day would start all over again. Once Helicant did tell the family the truth. In one of the more experimental incarnations of the day. She ranted and raved about who and what they were—it didn't end well.

No, something about Destiny's existence had caused an upheaval on the island. Her impossible girl created a stutter in time. They would live this way until she broke the curse for good.

"It changes nothing," she told him. "I want Drew dead."

Edward stopped pacing and stared at the floor. "He needs to be punished, but I'll leave that for Destiny to decide."

Helicant moved to get up and argue. This time, her feet were more firmly planted on the ground. She still needed to use the armrest of the fainting couch, but she otherwise stood tall. Helicant was not going to allow this.

"If he's not dead by dawn, I'll see you both dead."

Edward looked up at her with thick, furry brows, "You'll kill me the way you killed William?"

This made Helicant's knees buckle, forcing her to sit down. "How do you know that?"

"I understand why you did it. He wanted to send Destiny away. Was speaking to Carl about building a boat to sail to the mainland. He had spoken to me about taking her to a psychiatric ward."

"What makes you think I did it?"

"All the plants on this island are well documented," Edward explained. "A few generations ago, someone's child died eating them. Same symptoms."

Helicant wasn't sorry.

It was an unfortunate situation, but it was impossible to leave the island. William would've set sail with her daughter and got them both killed. Not just because of the curse but because he was no sailor and Carl was not a shipwright.

"William was going to paddle out to sea with my only child," Helicant said. "They wouldn't survive."

"He gave you no other option?"

Helicant turned away. William deserved a better wife; she knew that. There were many regrets in her life, but stopping her husband from shipping Destiny off into the unknown was not one of them.

"He blamed me for Destiny's ailments. Said she needed to get away from me. That may be true, but I wasn't going to let him punish her for my wrongs. Besides," Helicant said as she stood. "He really didn't have a say in the matter."

There was a long breath then. A question long unanswered, but there was no reason to keep it from him now.

"You're admitting it, then?"

Helicant found the will to move one foot in front of the other. Exhausted as she was, there would be no rest for her until she saw her sister's body.

"I'm going to wake Sophie," she said. "Dinner needs to be served. Even if no one is here."

"Helicant," Edward called.

She gave a deep sigh. Helicant Sallows had more than enough of this day. "Yes, Edward. Destiny is your child."

Coral

Coral marched out of the mansion and into the crisp night air. She was not afraid of the mist hovering over the ground so thick that she could no longer see her feet. She was not bothered by the unnerving silence of the island. She was not the least bit spooked by the fact that somewhere on this island, there was a crazed rapist who enjoyed torturing and murdering animals.

At least, this is what she told herself as she franticly fidgeted with the sewing kit in her pocket. The events of the night were more turbulent than the tides crashing into the island day in and day out. How could things go from such delirious joy to utter depravity within hours? Thank the gods Daniel had his wits about him.

Come to think of it, her son was rather heroic. Not just in how he rescued his bride, but in the way he responded to her. As if he knew on some instinctual level how to care for her, like Carl, but more dominant.

She had no doubt that something had happened. If Drew had a cave full of the things Edward described, he was likely capable of

Destiny's accusation. Why she was out there in the first place, Coral could never understand. She should have been in the house or, at the very least, chaperoned. Irresponsible behavior often leads men to the wrong conclusions, if Drew's conclusion was even wrong in the first place.

Perhaps Destiny was attempting to sabotage her engagement to Daniel by falling victim to Drew's advances. Or maybe the girl sought to escape the pressure by playing the victim to garner sympathy from her mother and cancel the marriage. Fortunately, Daniel found the damsel in distress just in time and had become the hero.

The dirt road that winded down the hillside to Coral's humble cottage was a long one. She could only assume that Carl went directly home and that Joseph found his father there and never bothered to come back. There were other conclusions that dawned in her mind, but she pushed them away. Carl was safe. Joseph was fine.

As she made her way down to sea level, the grass grew taller and wilder. Mud reverted to soil before sifting into sands underfoot. It was part of the reason why her home didn't hold up as well as the others. Between the salty winds and the shifting foundation, her home was more prone to the elements than the others.

Somewhere in the tall patches of grass, a pale hand blended in with the sand. She didn't notice it until it moved. Digits wriggling and grasping in Coral's direction made her scream and jump away. Blood thundered between her ears, and she slapped a hand over her screaming mouth.

A glint of gold shined in the moonlight. It was a plain gold band on a ring finger. She prayed for it to not be Carl's hand, but she knew in her heart that it was him. Coral silently cried as she approached the hand. The arm was half-buried in the sand. Kneeling, she uncovered her husband, who was lying face down.

He groaned as she rolled him over. Her loving husband. The best person she had ever known was half-conscious and struggling. His skin was raw and peeling all over. He reminded her of an unpeeled, boiled potato. Underneath the thin white shirt she had given him, Carl's skin was just as marred and angry. If it peeled away anymore, it would expose the muscle and very bone of her husband.

What could have caused this? He looked as though he was rotting alive. Helpless and afraid, Coral refused to let it show. "What are you doing, you ridiculous man?" she asked.

"It absorbed the moisture."

"What?"

"The sweat... It kept coming. It made my hands and feet prune. My skin grew so agitated with the constant damp that it began to peel. The sand was the only thing that kept me dry."

Coral couldn't understand what was happening. She looked around in the fleeting hope that Edward would be nearby with answers. It was just a skin infection, Coral told herself. She just needed to get to Beth or Edward, and they could make him better. They had to.

"Have you seen Joseph?" Coral asked.

Carl's eyes were still open, but he was no longer looking at her. His body was growing cold. Coral listened to the sound of her own breaths and synced them with the waves washing ashore. This couldn't be happening.

"Wake up," Coral told him. "Please."

She shoved at her husband's torso and noted there was the slightest bit of life still in him. His breath was dangerously shallow, and he was growing cold, but it was still there. Carl was still there. He wouldn't be for much longer if she didn't do something.

Her fingers once again found the thimble and the needle. The thread and the scissors. Coral didn't know how to make medicine or determine an illness, but she could sew his torn skin back together in hopes that it would prevent further damage.

Without a second thought, Coral produced the sewing kit from her pocket and threaded her needle. She used her scissors to cut away the damp clothing. His abrasions were most dangerous around the abdomen and chest area. His vital organs protruding, ready to spill out at any moment.

The shore was splashing against them, ridged and knocking, but Coral needed the salty water to wash away the sand before she repaired his skin. Ignoring her wet dress, Coral took her unconscious husband by the wrists and dragged him a safe distance away from the rushing water. He let out a groan of pain, and Coral realized his back was likely just as torn as his front.

"I'm sorry," she told him. "Once I get the front done, I can take care of the back."

Coral set to work on the worst parts. The places where blood-stained bone glimmered in the moonlight. Where muscle bulged and threatened to spill the contents onto the sand. She worked quickly and silently. Carl gave no indication that he minded.

When Coral finished with the front, she rolled him over onto the clean grass and used the severed clothes and seawater to wash away the sand on Carl's backside. Once he was sufficiently cleaned, Coral set to work once more. By the time she finished, her thread was gone, and her fingers stung.

"There," she said with confidence. "Better than ever."

Carl's eyelids were sewn open. She figured her husband would rather have them open than sewn shut. It did give him an eerie appearance, however. At some point, Coral had realized he was no longer breathing, but she couldn't bear the thought of her husband being dead, so she continued to sew.

Perhaps it was Coral's mind playing tricks on her, but when she finished, Carl was alive once again. He twitched against the freshly made seams along his body. Convulsing and discharging bile and fecal matter, Carl remained mobile even after he should have been dead.

Coral patted her husband's bare chest and kissed him on the face. "You'll never leave me now. Can you speak?" she asked him.

Carl opened his torn mouth and let out a wail of pain.

"Shh," she told him. "That's enough. Shh…"

Destiny

Destiny had never enjoyed someone's conversation the way she enjoyed Daniel's. He was bright, funny, but empathetic. She was still giggling from the story he told her about himself and Joseph trying to sneak a pie from the table.

"I suspect Mother knew something was amiss," he said. "We both walked into the house with our faces and hands stained with blackberry."

"Aww," Destiny laughed. "How much trouble did you get into?"

Daniel was looking over the books in Sophie's collection. Her library was smaller than the mansion's, but it was curated. All the books in her aunt's possession had to do with the history of Sallows Island. From genealogy to the journals of the first settlers.

"Enough. We picked blackberries all day the next day. Where does she keep Nathaniel's diary?"

Destiny had forgotten all about that book. She was about to explain that she had it in her coat pocket when Daniel turned and said, "There it is!"

That wasn't possible. It was in her bedroom in her coat pocket. She had taken it when she was here earlier in the day. How did it end up back here? All the dust was gone, too, but she didn't mention that to Daniel.

Had she imagined that she took the book? It had been such a long day that Destiny couldn't be certain.

His eyes found hers for a brief moment, and her heart pounded, and she felt dizzy. Daniel remembered her aversion and turned away before her symptoms got worse. "If you don't mind, I'd like to read this."

"Please, I don't mind. People try to avoid it, but I think if more were willing to discuss it, I would be better off."

"The Diary of Nathanial Sallows...which story is it that you..." Daniel trailed off, uncertain of which story she dreamt of.

"It's called The Green-Eyed Monster."

"Oh, that's rather self-explanatory." Daniel fumbled through the book until he found the page. He paused before glancing her way. Destiny's breath froze in her throat, and she swallowed back the instant alarm she felt.

She didn't fear fainting or causing a scene because it was just Daniel, so none of that mattered. Her whole life, Destiny perceived her phobia as a great, unscalable wall that would prohibit her from enjoying life. Yet here she was, married to someone with green eyes, growing stronger in their gaze.

Her body's response didn't abate, but she was more confident that this fear wouldn't be her undoing.

"The Green-Eyed Monster," Daniel started. "Just when we thought we had everything under control, to our horror, we discovered the basement door was once again opened. This was the third time. Someone was intentionally releasing the monsters from their purgatory.

"No one was killed this time, but we needed it to be the last time. My brothers and I took turns guarding the door. It was on my watch that it happened; the door opened from the inside. It wasn't a monster that was responsible for the deaths of my kin, but a man. He was an ordinary-looking man. Nothing monstrous about him except his deeds.

"I confronted him. I asked him if he knew what he was doing. If he knew the horrors he would unleash onto the world. The man grinned and nodded. I had come to learn a thing or two about the creatures born on this island. They were not inherently evil beings. They were tortured, demented souls, but not always aware of the damage they inflicted.

"This man knew what he was doing, and he enjoyed the suffering of others. He was a thing of evil. In the face of my double-barrel shotgun, the man came up the stairs quietly where me and the rest of my family restrained him and decided what to do with him.

"He lived on the island well before we arrived. He was either able to avoid the monsters, or they simply thought he was one of them. We tried to interrogate him, but the man enjoyed the beatings. With no satisfaction, I admit I got carried away on several occasions. All the while, he wouldn't say a single word.

"We kept him locked in one of the rooms in Sallows Hall, away from the main rooms, so the women couldn't hear his screams. Nothing frightened this man. The more fingernails we ripped off, the more excited he became. The more nails we drove through his hands and feet, the more he laughed. It became clear to us that his thing was not a man at all. He was a monster in the guise of a man."

Destiny was visibly shaking. Her teeth chattered, and her legs jerked as she struggled to maintain a slow and steady breathing pattern. She was tuning Daniel out and withdrawing into what she imagined to be her bedroom. It wasn't safer than any other place.

"Should I stop?" Daniel asked.

Destiny wanted to say yes. She wanted him to stop, but it was almost over. She shook her head no and said, "Go on."

"You sure?"

Destiny nodded and wrapped her hands around her chest to stop them from caving in.

"If it makes you feel any better, it's giving me the willies too," Daniel said.

She couldn't help but giggle, and in an instant, the spell was broken. The story couldn't hurt her. "I'm fine, really."

"The more we flogged, pierced, and ravaged his body, the more monstrous we became. Instead of dreaming of holding a woman in my arms, I dreamt of violence. My brothers and nephews and remaining son confessed to feeling the same way. Each day, we invented new ways to break an unbreakable man, and each day, we lost a little bit more of our humanity. All the while, those piercing green eyes mocked us.

"One day, we decided to not go back into the room. We left the man in there with no food or drink but kept a watchful eye on him. He paced and laughed to himself the first few days. After that, he began to pound on the door and scream. He tried to instigate our anger by giving us details of our loved one's deaths. We ignored him.

"After several weeks, it was apparent the man couldn't escape the room. One afternoon, my brother found that the green-eyed man had gouged out one of his eyes. He was already so badly scarred that he no longer resembled the man I caught in the basement, but he became so hideous that we stopped looking through the peephole altogether.

"The man grew thinner, uglier, and scar grew over scar, but even after months and months, he did not die. He always seemed to know when one of us was looking through the peephole because we always found his green eye glaring back at us. We decided, for everyone's sake, that it would be best if no one ever looked again. We walled off that hallway and built over it. His punishment for what he did to my family is to live an eternity alone.

Daniel closed the book and said nothing for several minutes. It allowed Destiny the time she desperately needed to recover. Leaning into Sophie's chair, she stayed warm by the fire. Allowing her mind to go blank as she stared into the flames.

"Is it as bad as you remember?"

"It's different, I suppose," Destiny said. "The things that I once found frightening seem to have lost their touch, and new aspects of the story have taken their place."

"There's a lot to be upset about in that story." Daniel was peeking out of the lead-lined glass windows as he spoke.

"I used to think that the part about the man enjoying torture was scary, what he did to himself. But now, the idea of spending eternity alone seems scarier."

He smiled then as if he felt the same. He had nice teeth, but they were normal nice teeth, not glaringly bright like Drew's. Daniel had more of a humble smile that eased the nausea roiling in her belly.

"Oh, look there," he said, pointing over Destiny's head.

She turned around and looked up at the mantle but didn't know what he was talking about. Daniel approached some books on the shelf pressed together with bookends. The left side was the front half of an arrow, and the right was the other half.

"The broken arrow bookends?" That was what she always called them as a child when she stayed the night.

"Yes, except it's not a bookshelf at all." Daniel moved the bookend with the arrow, and the whole thing came with it. It was a hidden booze compartment.

"I saw Edward take the whiskey decanter out of a similar one in your drawing room, except the one in the drawing room has a naked woman on each side."

She knew the piece and never thought to investigate it further. "I've never tried to read the books on that shelf because they were duplicates of the books in the library."

"I bet your mother made you read those first."

She did. Destiny laughed as Daniel offered her the small green glass decanter hidden behind the fake books. "Don Quixote isn't that long."

Daniel seated himself on the worn carpet on the floor, and they took turns sipping off the decanter. It was strong, whatever it was. The liquid smelled like spice and burned her throat. Destiny was never much of a drinker to begin with, but Daniel didn't seem all that enthusiastic either. He fought back a bitter expression and hastily passed the bottle back to her.

"Not into drinking either?" she asked her future husband.

He shook his head. "I like beer, but I've only ever had it the one time."

Destiny knew what he was talking about. She took another sip and sucked on her tongue. "My mother called it the hops conspiracy."

"Oh, you heard about it, then?"

Destiny forced back a smile, but it failed. "I heard that the small crop of hops died under 'mysterious circumstances' and that all the men drank the last of the ale as if they were attending a funeral."

Daniel's chuckle was sweet and contagious. "Edward was rather upset. We all got quite drunk that night. The next morning my head hurt something fierce."

"Nothing has grown there since." Destiny knew her mother suspected Beth was behind it since she had the greatest motivation to put an end to the ale brewing. Destiny never got a chance to taste it. She wondered if she'd ever get that chance.

"Probably nothing ever will." Daniel stared into the fire. Destiny looked at him, and he shied away. "He watered the hops with seawater."

"Who did?"

"Drew."

The name lingered in the room like an unwanted guest. Destiny took another hearty swig, and it made her feel just a little bolder. "Why would he do that?"

"I'm not sure, but I saw him do it. It was early in the morning, and he was out there, pouring a bucket of water on the vines. After one, he marched off to the shore and got another and another. Never felt the need to confront him on it; he's rather unpredictable at times."

Destiny was inclined to agree with that. He was always the one instigating the games where someone got hurt when they were children. Nothing outright cruel or out of the ordinary. He and Abigail fought a lot, but that was it.

"Edward must have made him very angry."

"That was my conclusion," Daniel said, pulling out the diary again. "Have you read any of the other stories?"

Destiny shook her head. She was giddy with alcohol and probably the idea of being alone with a boy for as long as she had. Destiny stared at him until he looked her way, and she then flinched and laughed at her own panic.

"Do you want to?"

Daniel's throat bobbed in response to her question, and something like mischief took hold of Destiny.

Sophie

There was a pattering on her cheek. Not in a hard or painful manner, merely a persistent slapping. She opened her eyes to a woman who strongly resembled her sister twenty years ago. Her eyes were wider without the heavy fold of the eyelids, fully revealing the chaotic streams of color woven throughout her hazel eyes. Her hair was darker and softer than before. Still streaked with grey but less so. The countless fine lines around her lips were gone. It was as if the sharp ridges along her cheeks and forehead had picked up the slack of her aging skin.

"Helicant?"

"Are you going to get up, or are you content with making me wait?"

It was Helicant all right. Sophie's eyes were going, but not so much that her older sister would suddenly appear younger than she was. There was something else different but familiar all the same. That wasn't so strange. She knew every version of her sister, after all.

"Well?"

All at once, Sophie remembered the last fleeting image of what made her faint to begin with. Her eyes welled with tears, and her voice cracked as she spoke. "She's dead."

There was pain in her sister's eyes; Sophie could see it. A quiet rage and the slight tremble of Helicant's lip gave her away.

She gave a stiff nod. "We have to get her out of there."

Sophie realized what she meant. The squeak of the kitchen doors revealed Edward. Both sisters looked at him. "She can't remain down there."

Edward didn't seem to understand, but Helicant was teetering on the edge of shouting. "I think it would be best if we wait till tomorrow to deal with the remains."

"We can't leave Beth down there!" Helicant shouted. She was clutching her hands together so hard that her knuckles were turning white.

"Edward, Beth was terrified of the basement," Sophie explained. To his credit, Edward didn't flinch at Helicant's rage. He was so disheveled and bewildered. His suit appeared too small for him, puckering at the seams, and his beard bristled along his face and neck.

"You could use a hot meal," he said. "How about we have Sophie send up the food in the dumbbell waiter, and I'll take care of Beth?"

"What will you do with her?" Sophie asked.

"I can move her into the laundry room. No one goes in there."

There was no telling how Helicant felt about it, but she didn't object. Edward wanted to assist her up to the dining room, but she swatted him away when he tried to follow her. "Get away from me," she told him. "Do right by your wife."

Edward let out an exhausted sigh. "Okay, I will get the wheelbarrow."

Sophie trotted to the side of the house and unpinned several linens. They were once dry, but the evening air had dampened them once more. That was okay; Beth wouldn't feel the damp anymore. From where the clotheslines were strung, she could see the dim lights of her cottage as well as smoke from the chimney. Sophie wished it was her that was in there, curled up with a good book and some tea.

Wadding up the blankets in her arms, Sophie brought them to Edward, who had dumped the extras from the wheelbarrow onto the ground. "We will be changing her into a white gown for the funeral anyhow," Sophie said.

Edward hesitated when she tried to follow him down. "You should let me cover the body first."

"I want to see her." It still rang in her head over and over that Beth was dead. Just when it felt as though the idea had settled, she'd think it again and find herself in a state of shock all over again.

Edward gave a stern turn of his head. "I don't think that's a good idea, Sophie. It's not a pretty sight. It wasn't a natural death."

There were images in her mind just then. Of her sister bent and broken, of her face being horribly disfigured. Sophie needed to know the truth of those visions, but she didn't want to force her way into what must have been a terrible situation for Edward.

"I remember bits from before I fainted," she said, twisting her fingers in her hand. "I know she's your wife, but she's my twin."

Edward pulled her into his embrace and kissed her forehead. "All right, but if you feel as though you are to faint again..."

Sophie broke from his arms and nodded without looking at him. Was he so quick to move on? Her sister's body was barely cold. Taking the lantern from the nail in the wall, Sophie lit the wick with the fire from the oven and gave Edward a hard look. He waited by the basement door, linens now in hand.

If anyone had told her that tonight would end this way, Sophie would've just as soon stayed home. She led the way down the steps and tried her best to not look at the place where her sister was left dead.

She made it to the basement steps where she waited, but to Sophie's confusion and horror, Beth wasn't there. Wondering if her mind was playing tricks on her, Sophie turned to Edward at the platform on the steps. His mouth was slack as he stared at the same spot.

"Where is she?" Sophie stammered.

Edward looked around as if he expected to find that Beth had moved to a different spot in the basement. A discrepancy in their collective memory or a miscalculation, perhaps. Neither had happened. Beth's body was just gone.

Sophie jerked her sights from the vacant spot on the dirt floor to Edward and back at the area again as if she thought the body would suddenly reappear. "What is the meaning of this?"

"I don't know."

"Edward!"

"I don't know, dammit, I don't know."

Edward paced the area and motioned for her to come closer. Sophie hesitated at first, but then she remembered that she was the one with the lamp in her hand. The lamp rattled as she moved closer—the only noise in the room.

Sophie watched as Edward kneeled and observed the ground. "No sign of her or the puddle."

"Puddle?"

"Helicant broke a bottle. Made a mess of her hand and spilled wine everywhere. Beth had died in the same spot Helicant had dropped the wine."

The basement floor was dirt, but even dirt wouldn't be able to absorb a full bottle of wine and return to an arid state. There was no stain at all. Sophie wondered if Edward could have been mistaken. She didn't remember seeing the stain, but she did remember seeing her sister's corpse. Beth was dead.

"She's dead," Sophie whispered.

"Yes, she is dead, but where did she go?"

Sophie felt as though she heard a whisper and turned around. There was nothing there, just the door to the catacombs. That ugly old door glared back at Sophie, and she couldn't help but wonder if her sister was in there somehow.

Two strong hands grasped Sophie by the shoulders. "Sophie, no!"

Her hand was on the doorknob. How did she get there? Sophie turned to look at Edward for an explanation. She could only shake her head in denial. "I..."

"Let's get upstairs."

While she fully agreed, Edward didn't give her a chance to say otherwise. He practically pulled her up the steps and back into the kitchen and what felt like reality. "I'm fine. Stop."

"You were about to open the door," he said.

"I don't remember doing it."

Sophie took a breath and straightened herself out. She couldn't explain what was happening. Helicant's face, her sister's body... The basement. They'd always feared that place as children; it seemed fitting that they'd meet their end in the cellar. Perhaps that was what Sophie wanted the most. She and Beth entered this world together, so it only made sense they'd departed at the same time.

"You should check on Helicant. I'm going to wheel dinner up."

"Are you sure you are all right?"

"I'm fine," she promised, but she just remembered once again that Beth was dead. The kitchen seemed so much bigger than before. More than anything, Sophie just wanted to be left alone for a while.

"I'll be just up the stairs if you need me."

Sophie watched the double doors swing as he left. She waited until they had become completely still and Edward's footfalls were no longer heard before she fell to the floor and wept. She allowed herself a full, unadulterated cry and made no attempt to hide her anguish.

When the heaving and tears subsided, Sophie remained on the ground for a few minutes more to gather her composure. Before her mind could tell her, Sophie reminded herself that her sister had passed on.

Coming to a stand, Sophie rolled up her sleeves and pushed up the door to the dumbbell waiter. It was a stiff, heavy door, and she was worried she wouldn't be able to push it open on her own. They really ought to have had a different design for this thing, but she supposed it was too late now.

Green beans and roasted chicken were the first to go in. Sophie gave the box a knock, and Edward pulled the cart upward. After a few minutes, she pulled the rope, and the box came downward in jerking movements. She hoped the gravy wouldn't spill.

The best solution was to buttress the gravy between the potatoes, carrots, and rolls. She gave a knock, and there was no response. It was no matter. With both hands, Sophie pushed the box up a foot to grab hold of the rope and pull the cart up.

She left the box at their level to go back for the pie. It was a berry pie. Beth loved berry pie. Her sister loved pie in general, but wild berry was her favorite. Sophie used to make it every year for her birthday until the year Beth refused to let her in the house.

"Just go away," Beth said from behind her front door. "I don't want to see anyone today."

"It's your birthday, and I made you this pie." Was it something she had done, or rather didn't do? They had grown apart in their age. Beth always wanted to be Sophie's other half until the day Edward married her.

This time it was different. Beth wasn't pushing her away because she finally held superiority over Sophie. It wasn't a trivial fight; Sophie hadn't taken Helicant's side, and Beth hadn't been caught gossiping. Her twin just wouldn't see her.

"Please, Beth," Sophie said against the door. "I know we've grown up, but I made this for you, and I miss you. Please open the door."

There was a moment's hesitation. Sophie was certain that Beth would forgive her for whatever had happened, but then Beth said, "Just go away, Sophie. Go away like you always do."

There were no more wild berry pies for Beth's birthday after that. It had been years since that day. Sophie never thought to ask what she had done to anger Beth so. She supposed she'd never know now.

She took the pie to the empty cart in the dumbbell waiter. She slid the ceramic pie dish into the box and pushed the ceiling of the box up, but it wouldn't budge. The device was so old and so seldom used that the wheels struggled to turn.

The damn thing was off track. There was some give, but she'd need both hands to give it a good shove. Reaching halfway into the device, she wiggled the box in hopes that it would slide back in place. Shuttering the whole contraption, the door didn't budge.

Just a little bit more, and she'd have it.

There was a click as if the cart had fallen into place, which was good because Sophie didn't think she could go another round with the dumbwaiter. She gave one small wiggle to the box and approved of the way it swayed on the rope. Just like it was supposed to. It would work better than it had in years by her estimation.

The outer door fell.

A deft crunch sounded before Sophie registered what had happened. Then came the pain. Reverberating from her elbows and up her arms, her throat clammed shut, and her knees gave out. Kneeling before the altar of agony, Sophie's arms dislocated at the shoulders as her dead weight slumped to the floor.

All wore black on this day because it was the end of days...

Destiny

She longed to be closer to him. Despite being married, there was still the habit of worrying about what the others would think. More importantly, what would her mother think? She dismissed the notion. Destiny wore the ring now. If her mother or anyone else wanted to frown on her actions, they shouldn't have given her the ring.

Slipping off the overstuffed chair, Destiny giggled and plopped beside her husband. His face was red from the heat of the fire and the drink, but now it had even more reason to be red. She managed to avoid his eyes the entire time.

"Read that one," she said, leaning over his arm to point at the diary.

"The Cannibal?"

"Mmhmm."

"We first encountered the cannibal under the full hunter's moon. We had just come ashore after a month of traveling by ship. Our nerves frayed and our stomachs still bobbing, we set out to find monsters, and we found her instead.

"She was a small creature with long black hair. More akin to Fae than any monster. Her sharp features and soft, bare skin lured us. Beckoned to her fire, she danced and sang. I didn't hesitate to break my vows that night. None of the men did. In the morning, we woke in the cold light of day and were forced to go home and confess to our wives what had happened.

"The women went out that night, thinking her to be a siren. I pleaded for my pregnant daughter to stay home, she was full with child, but the women ignored my request—still angry with our sins. I don't know just what befell the women, but there was a great fire in the woods that night. When the women returned home, they had the cannibal in chains. My daughter returned childless."

"Are you okay?" Daniel asked her.

Destiny wasn't sure why she wouldn't be. She looked at him and instantly regretted it. One glance and she was drowning. No matter how deeply she inhaled, her breaths could not satisfy. Her head swam in panic, unsure of where to find safety.

"Sorry. Habit."

Destiny needed to reposition herself. She crawled along the floor and laid down on her belly. "I'm okay," she told him. "Just need a minute."

Together, they listened to the crackle of the fire. She thought she could hear screaming. "Did you hear screaming?"

"I don't think so."

"Read some more."

"The women folk put her in the catacombs, naked and laughing. Our wives and daughters were slow to forgive our discretions. One of the nights the green-eyed monster opened the catacomb door, it was the cannibal that escaped. She lured my son into the forest, where he was never seen again.

"We only know her to be a cannibal because when we tracked her down once more, we found nothing but a child on a heap of bones. It was undoubtedly her, as if consuming human flesh made her younger. It also made her more powerful. She could move things with her mind and told us how we were going to die as we carried the child into the catacombs once more.

"The second and last time she got out, we found her eating parts of the stillborn baby she had fermenting in a clay jar. In the end, the cannibal caused her own undoing. Reduced to a helpless toddler, she had no memory of her former self."

"It doesn't say where they put her."

Daniel considered the thought but kept his eyes mindfully on the page. "It doesn't. I always thought the Sallows got rid of all the monsters, but it seems like they couldn't kill most of them."

"We were children," Destiny rationalized. "Our parents told us the monsters were gone so we'd sleep at night, just as their parents told them."

It also didn't mean that any of these creatures were real. She doubted anyone could kill the monsters in their own minds. For whatever reason, the family came here. They struggled and toiled for what was probably nothing. It must've been so hard, losing loved ones to things they didn't understand.

Destiny knew better than anyone that monsters were easier than just being messed up in the head.

"Daniel," she said, "Do you suppose that map is the one they mention in the story?"

"You mean the green-eyed monster?"

Destiny got up and had a closer look at the map. "They said they built over the wing where the room is and that they didn't update the map."

Daniel didn't say anything.

"I wonder if the room is actually there."

Daniel winced. "Now why would you want to go and find it?"

Destiny was surprised by his reaction. "You're a man of science. If we find there is no room, then my dream is not real."

"What if there is a room?" Daniel asked.

She couldn't help but smile. "Are you afraid?"

"Sort of," he admitted. "You've come so far just in the few hours we've spent together. You're avoiding my face less and less by the minute. I think if we find a room, even if there's no monster, it will confirm your fears, and it will make things worse."

It had occurred to her. She was pushing herself so hard today, and she was exhausted by the spikes of fear, but she also felt emboldened by it. Experiencing an actual threat like she had with Drew made her want to confront the fears that lurked in the shadows. The ones that had never harmed her but still gripped her mind.

"I want to find it," she told him. Destiny knew he wouldn't say no. He loved her too much to tell her no. He let out a sigh and raised his head to the ceiling as if he were muttering a prayer.

"We really have to do this? Can we just wait a little while longer? Until we know for sure where Drew is?"

Destiny supposed she could wait a while longer. "But only if you read more stories."

"Okay," Daniel said. "How about The Zombie?"

"No." Destiny's face scrunched with the sound of that one. Knowing she had won, Destiny plopped down by the fire and took a few more sips of alcohol while Daniel began to read.

"The Gargoyle. Out of all the creatures on the island, the gargoyle was the most docile despite its ugliness. Its short, compact body was barrel-chested with stringy arms and bowed legs. Its head was large and held a misshapen face that creased with thick lines that imitated that of a man's. It had great big talons on its hands and feet and horns that spiraled unevenly from its head. It has wings, but the body was too heavy, making it nearly flightless.

"As far as we could tell, it was harmless. My niece nearly ran into the beast while trying to pen the chickens one evening. She said she screamed, and the thing fell over and scrambled to get away. None of the chickens were harmed. There was some debate on what to do with it. Some of the family wanted to leave it alone; others wanted to catch it.

"Ultimately, we decided to leave it alone. It was not dangerous. If anything, it was a creature that roused our sympathy. We had already taken so many losses.

"Sometimes, at night, it can be seen hobbling around the yard. It stares into the water in the well only to lash out at its own reflection. There is something so human in its self-loathing. It didn't ask to be born a hideous beast. None of us are."

Abigail

Abigail got off the bare mattress and searched the ground for her dress. She found it in a pile beside his boots. She was about to put it back on when the bright light of the moon distracted her. Stepping into the light, her body looked as though it were glowing.

"Beautiful," Drew whispered.

She glanced back at him with a knowing smile. The view was lacking, Abigail admitted, but the window was able to frame the moon just right. Hands slid around her belly, and she felt a nibble at her ear.

"Let's stay here a little bit longer," Drew said.

Abigail bowed her head. "I need to check on Destiny. Last I saw her, she had fainted."

"She's fine. Trust me, I know."

"How would you know?" Abigail pulled away. Feeling exposed all of a sudden, she wrapped her arms over her breasts and stared at him. "When did you see her last?"

Drew shifted, and his demeanor was that of a whipped dog. He wouldn't look her in the eyes, and he was struggling to explain something.

"Drew, you said you scared her. Just what did you do?"

"I just chased her around a little," he stammered. "I didn't touch her. I swear. She's a fast one, our cousin. I thought I knew that maze, but not like her."

Abigail felt her stomach sink. He didn't touch her. He chased her. She understood why he did it, but she never thought to ask what he would have done if he had caught her. "If you had caught her?" Abigail asked.

Drew shook his head and extended his arms out. "I didn't intend on it."

He flashed that perfect smile of his, and Abigail knew he was lying. He only did that when he lied. "Get out," she barked at him. "I never want to see you again."

"Abi—"

"Get out!" She screamed, pointing at the door. Swiping her dress from the ground, she clutched it to her naked body. Abigail didn't want him to see her anymore. She was wrong to sleep with him. She was willing to overlook his flaws if it meant getting back at Edward for not wanting her, but any danger towards Destiny wasn't worth it.

Drew dressed hurriedly and bolted out the door with his shoes still in his hand. The door shut with a resounding click. Abigail felt sick. She rubbed her hand on her face and turned away from the damned spotlight in the window. How could he lie to her?

No. He didn't lie. She just didn't want to know.

Moving to pull her dress over her head, Abigail was suddenly overrun with dizziness. A firm hand grabbed her arm, and she spun around to hit Drew with her free hand, except no one was there. She was the only one in the room, and the nothingness on her arm was cool to the touch. The room lost all the magic it once held and was nothing more than a haunted shell of regret.

Abigail slipped the dress on and went to grab her shoes from the floor when she was pushed to the ground. She looked behind her to see that Drew was standing there. He no longer wore the façade. His face was cold and mocking as he undid his belt.

"What are you doing?" She shouted, turning around to grab a shoe. When Abigail looked back to throw it, no one was there. The shoe slapped against a bed with a naked mattress, and dust clouds bloomed in the air.

Abigail, still on her hands and knees, didn't understand what was happening to her. Someone—Drew—was attacking her. It was likely what he had in store for Destiny had she not escaped.

But Drew wasn't here. No one was here but her.

Her dress was thrown over her head. Abigail cried out for help as rough fingers dug into her hips. Her face went hot with anger as she was violated. She pulled forward abruptly, slipping away from her attacker before swinging a leg in his direction. Her leg hit air as she once again found herself alone.

Not entirely alone.

Abigail felt eyes on her, and the moonlight illuminated an odd shape in the window. She looked up from the floor and saw a beast handing upside down like a bat, red eyes glowing. Abigail let out a shriek, and the creature lost its footing and fell from view.

Fleeing from the room, she ignored the wet sensation dripping between her thighs. There was a monster. A real, bloody monster, just like the book spoke of. The stories were real, she couldn't believe it, but they were real.

Running down the steps to the first floor, Abigail burst through the kitchen doors to find Sophie—dead and strung up by her elbows caught in the dumbbell waiter. She let out a scream and ran from that damned mansion and into the garden sobbing hysterically.

It was dark except for the moonlight, but Abigail didn't care. She could scarcely see in front of her from all the tears in her eyes anyways. She was going off of memory of the maze from when she and Destiny were young. It wasn't a great recollection, but she needed solitude.

Perhaps Sophie wasn't dead, and rather, she'd just fainted. Though Abigail didn't think so. All color was drained from her face. It looked as though she had been there for some time. Where was everyone? Abigail ran into a hedge, mistaking it for a way through. She hit and slapped at the bush until her knuckles stung from the myriad of tiny scratches.

The hedge maze cut some of the wind, but Abigail was shivering violently. Her silk dress did nothing to keep the wind from pelting at her skin. Her hair had fallen from her updo in thick tendrils, which she only noticed when she was wiping her wet, sore face.

Monsters were real.

She saw one. They all thought the stories were legends or exaggerations of what really took place when Nathanial Sallows and his family arrived on the shores of the island. It couldn't all be true. How could they make such a grand house with so few people while being constantly attacked by monsters?

Abigail's theory was that the island was once a thriving community, dried up by lack of trade or some such. No monsters, just rough oceans and dwindling coin. So many books told of civilizations falling into ruin, it never occurred to her that there was any truth to the family saga.

Kicking up the fog as she navigated the maze, Abigail came to a clearing that she recognized. The center of the maze with its moss-covered fountain overflowing with fetid water.

She seated herself on the swing, but she didn't feel like swinging. More horrible things had happened to her in the last hour than they had in her whole life. Before this evening, the worst things to happen were rumors that she was sleeping with Edward and her mother's incessant need to see her married.

She wished she were Edward's mistress. Maybe then she wouldn't have felt the need to get his attention by sleeping with his son, followed by being raped by an apparition of his son. Or whatever that was. Abigail wasn't certain what had transpired.

Deep down, she had understood on some level. The attack was a haunting of what might've happened. Had she not been so desperate, he would have found a way to exact his revenge. If not on her, then on Destiny or anyone else who stood in his way.

At the heart of it, Drew wanted to claim the dominance that his father held over the island. His father had courted the twins and Helicant in his time. Drew felt entitled to the same sort of stud mentality, but neither she nor Destiny showed any interest.

Drew's seed dried along her thigh, and it was beginning to itch. It stuck to the thin, baby hairs of her inner thigh and pulled at them when she moved. In her irritation, Abigail hiked up her dress and scratched at it with her nails until her skin was searing.

Her nails raked along the delicate skin until she lifted her head and cried out in pain. The crust underneath her nails smelled salty and stale. Abigail rushed to the fountain and plunged her hands into the stagnant water. Anything would be better than their current state. The water smelled strange enough on its own, but it wasn't bad. Better than Drew's stench.

There was no one out there but her. No one would see. She slipped out of her dress and sat on the edge of the fountain, dipping her feet into the waters blackened by night. She cupped the water with her hands and splashed it on her legs. Abigail's toes wiggled against the slimy fountain floor. The water was warmer than she'd thought it would be, considering the time of year.

Abigail slipped into the fountain pool. Submerged up to her waist, the cold sting of the wind and the guilt that seemed to constantly hover over her head seemed to lessen. She washed herself with the fetid water and marveled at how the moisture clung to her like a second skin.

Without a second thought, she laid back in the water. She allowed it to fully cover everything except her face, which surfaced like a pale moon in the night sky. In the water, she felt clean. Abigail no longer cared about Edward, about the monster, Drew, or her mother. All that anger and suffering seemed to fade away to a distant memory, or perhaps it was something that happened to someone else.

Abigail felt herself become one with the water. She didn't know where her body ended or where the water began. She could feel the edges of the fountain and the metal drain at the bottom. This was once the main source of fresh water for the island. She could go anywhere the water flowed. Her eyes opened, and she took one last look at the night sky before submerging what remained of Abigail in the water.

Coral

Coral led her husband home. He was sluggish, and she had to help him most of the way. His skin no longer peeled, and the stitches seemed to be holding, but his skin was turning an unhealthy color. She noticed his fingers and eyelids were blackening. A thick, angry purple vein was crawling along his chest.

"Just sit there," she said as she pushed the heap onto a chair. She went into the kitchen to wash her hands. Coral used the scrub brush that she reserved for scouring the pots underneath her fingers. Just when she thought her hands were clean, another grain of sand embedded itself in the skin under the nail.

Turning around to check on Carl, she had to pinch her lips together to keep from crying. He was just staring at the wall. His eyeballs protruded weirdly as his eyelids shrank away. Coral tore her gaze from her husband and began putting things away in the kitchen. She had left it such a mess when they left. Clearly, she was distracted by her son's wedding.

There was no sign of Joseph or Daniel. There was a pang of guilt when she realized she didn't include Abigail in that thought. She loved her daughter, and if anyone could help, it would be Abigail. Coral wished she could tell her how sorry she was. She was just intimidated by her daughter's ambitions. A woman doctor was new and strange. Coral was raised to believe a woman's purpose was singular. Helicant changed all that when she became the matron, but this old girl still carried the opinions of the dead.

The sound of a chair being pushed along the floor stopped Coral's kitchen arranging. She looked around the corner and saw that he was no longer there. "Carl? She called.

There was no answer. Coral turned and came face to face with what used to be her husband. His eyes budged from their sockets, and his lips were shrinking away from his teeth save the places she had sewn. His skin was swollen and uneven, giving him a gruesome appearance. Coral couldn't help but gag and stumble back.

"There you are," she stammered. "Do you want something to eat?"

Carl reached for her with decaying hands and bloody fingernails. His mouth opened wide and exposed a shriveled tongue wagging inside a mouth of purple gums and long teeth. He meant to bite her. Why wouldn't her legs move? She cried out as he fell forward, his dull teeth making purchase.

A deep, piercing pain surged through Coral's shoulder and was enough to jar her legs into moving. She flailed and fought the monster, but it was too strong, and she only injured herself more when she struggled. His jaw was locked, and he was gnawing. She spotted a cast iron skillet and reached for it.

The teeth closed deeper on her shoulder. Coral's clavicle snapped like a sparrow's leg as the muscles were shorn from her shoulder. The most sensitive areas are always considered a delicacy. Any movement only increased the pain, but if she didn't grab that skillet, she would be dead soon.

With a roar, Coral jerked toward the skillet, ignoring the agony. Her hands were slippery with sweat, but she was close enough. Coral grabbed hold of the handle and swung the pan as hard as she could. The blow to the monster's head was enough to release his jaw.

She didn't quite bash the skull in, but there was now a solid dent where his ear once was. The jaw had unhinged, but Coral still had to push the monster off and wriggle free of its grasp. It was stunned enough that she was able to break free. She made a run for the door and into the darkness, but she could hear it dragging its feet after her.

Winded and straining, she was never the most athletic woman, and the corset constricted the air she needed to keep up. The sand beneath her feet didn't do her any favors either. Her throat burned, and her heart hammered. She had to stop running, or she would faint. At least then, she'd be unconscious when he ate her. Salvation was a small shed that her husband had built for her to sew and work on her taxidermy.

Falling through the door, Coral closed it behind her and slumped to the ground. Her weight barred the monster from entry. There were windows it could break through if it were capable of thought, but she would need to deal with that if it happened. After several silent minutes, it seemed the creature had given up. She wasn't about to check to see if it had, but it gave Coral a few minutes of reprieve.

The wound on her shoulder was hemorrhaging blood, and a black bile coated the torn flesh. Looking down, she could see the collarbones jutting out from where the monster bit. It was a miracle that she remained conscious after such an attack. Perhaps she was stronger than she realized.

What had she done? What had become of her poor Carl? It pained Coral to think she had done something so awful to her husband. What else could she have done? He was dying. It seemed that her Carl had died in any case, so there was a good chance he would have become that thing even if she hadn't sewn him back together.

Coral wept silently as she thought about how Carl would never see Daniel married. How they would never watch Joseph grow into maturity. They would never see their only daughter become the doctor she was determined to be. They'd never have that fine room alone together in the mansion and watch their grandchildren play in the maze. He deserved these things more than she ever did.

The pain in her shoulder throbbed and burned. She felt chilled and knew it to be shock. She would die in her craft shed, of all places, if she didn't come up with a plan to save herself.

"Okay, Coral," she said. "If you ever plan on telling Abigail that you're sorry and moving into that big old house, you had better get your shit together."

Once again, her fingers found the sewing kit in her pocket. She used her good arm to scoot to her basket of thread, where she grabbed the nearest one. With one arm nearly immobile, Coral struggled to thread the needle. She cursed each time the thread failed to enter the eye. After licking the end of the string, she was finally able to string her needle and set to work.

Big, fat drops of sweat fell from Coral's forehead, and her hand trembled between shock and the anticipation of more pain. On the table, an owl stared at her with its great yellow eyes as it perched on a small log. It was to be Daniel's wedding gift. Drew had found it in one of his traps. It sadly passed away before he got a chance to free the bird. Since it was still fresh and fully intact, Coral decided to taxidermy it.

The needle worked its way through her skin and didn't hurt all that much. Perhaps her shoulder was going numb from the blood loss or the shock—Coral couldn't say for certain, but sewing herself back together wasn't nearly as bad as she imagined. It didn't feel great, but in comparison to a monster bite, it wasn't too much to endure.

Coral was going to live.

One way or another, with or without Carl. Just when she had her shoulder sewn up, the door began to open. She let out a yelp of pain as she fell back on her bad arm to crawl away from the door. Coral looked around for something to defend herself with, but there was nothing but a few stuffed animals.

"Aunt Coral?" Drew whispered.

Coral was so relieved she couldn't speak. She could only shutter and stare at her savior. His eyes fell to her injury. "Come on," he approached and helped her up by her good arm. Together, they left the shop and made their way up the hill and towards the mansion.

"How did you find me?" She asked.

"I wasn't trying to."

Coral looked at him with a frown, wondering what on earth he meant by that. Drew lolled his head and told his secret. "I had built myself a makeshift boat. It was hidden near the shore. I was going to take it and get the hell out of here, but I found the boat smashed. I was coming back up the hill when I saw that thing chase you into the shed."

"Thank you."

"Don't thank me yet," Drew told her. "I'm being hunted."

"By who?" Coral asked.

"More like what."

Coral tried to put on a brave front. She felt much safer with Drew, but the evening had worn her thin. She sniffed back the tears while Drew supported her with his arm around her waist. "I don't think I can take anymore whats."

Drew looked like his father at that moment. Same determined gaze that scanned the horizon. "Let's just get to the manor first."

Coral wiped her eyes and nodded in agreement. If anyone could fix her shoulder, it would be Edward. He was probably still celebrating at the house with everyone else. It brightened her mood and made her feet feel lighter to think that everyone was still residing in the safety of the drawing room, but as the incline grew steeper, Coral's feet struggled.

She fell to the ground, and Drew helped her back to her feet. When she fell a second time, he growled with annoyance.

"I just need a moment," Coral said as she tried to catch her breath.

Drew surveyed the land all around them, "You're not going to make it to the manner."

"I'm fine."

Like a caged bird inside a burning house. She knew that whatever Drew had in mind was not in her best interest. She was suddenly reminded of the last conversation she had with her family in the drawing room. Destiny had accused Drew of trying to rape her. And the things Edward described when he discovered Drew's cave...

"We're closer to the forest," Drew said. "I know a nice, safe place where nothing will harm you. I'll go get Father and bring him to you."

"Why were you trying to flee the island in the night?" Coral asked.

Drew didn't answer. Coral struggled to her feet. "I'll manage on my own. You go on ahead without me."

"I can't leave you out here."

Drew took her by her good arm and led her toward the forest. Coral tried to fight back, but he slapped her shoulder, and the pain brought her to her knees and took the breath from her lungs. As her nephew drug her to his cave in the forest, Coral went limp, making it difficult for him to drag her. For once in her life, she was grateful for being on the heavier side.

"You've inspired me, Coral."

She gazed up at him, wondering just what he was getting at. The forest's edge was gone, and now the moonlight was obstructed by trees. Leaves crinkled underfoot, and Drew's boots stomped the forest with great authority. Coral didn't have the strength to fight, unwilling to endure any more attacks to her injury.

Drew was strong, but even he grew tired. He dropped her on the ground and walked around her, opting to drag Coral by her feet instead. She grabbed at things with her good arm, but he tugged harder, and she was forced to let go.

"I've been creating similar things in private."

Coral didn't answer him. Whatever he had in mind, she would've preferred to be eaten alive by her husband's corpse.

"Drew, I'm your aunt," she pleaded. "I changed your diapers as a baby. I held you when you fell and scrapped your knee. You're friends with my son."

He stopped for a moment. Spun around in panic and swiped his hand through his rust-colored hair as if he suddenly came to his senses. This was her chance to reason with him.

"Please, I won't tell anyone."

"It doesn't matter what you tell or don't. They've already decided they'll hang me for Destiny. Maybe Abby too...I..."

"Abigail?" Losing all sense of self-preservation, Coral had to know. "What did you do to my little girl?"

The battle for Drew's conscience was lost. The part of Drew that wanted to hurt her took over. He smiled devilishly at Coral. "She might have enjoyed it. I can't remember."

Coral felt the grip on her boots once more as Drew continued to take her deep into the forest. A renewed strength came over her as she realized that her daughter might be in trouble. She screamed as loudly as she could, hoping to get anything's attention, be it human or monster. Coral screamed until her voice went horse and her cries echoed within a cave.

Helicant

Sitting at her usual place at the head of her table, Helicant sipped on water and waited as Edward carved up the chicken with a large chef knife and a fork. His hands had grown even hairier. As tempting as it was to point it out, she'd wait until a more vexing time to point it out. A blade isn't sharpened by a whetstone so much as intent.

"What piece do you want?" Edward asked.

"Destiny loves the thighs, so save at least one for her. Sophie and Beth both prefer the breast, but Sophie cannot finish a whole one. They will probably split one."

Edward gave her a soft smile. "I asked you what piece you wanted."

"I'm not hungry. Not for chicken, at least."

"Potatoes and beans then?"

He wouldn't quit unless she ate something. Edward would start lecturing while heaping the vegetated slop on her plate. Not everything was worth fighting over. "I'll take a little of both, thank you."

He placed her plate in front of her before serving himself small servings. Edward seated himself in the chair beside Helicant's. "The rolls must be on their way."

Helicant forced herself to eat the food. It was tasteless and had the most disagreeable textures. Why hadn't they slaughtered one of the pigs? For a feast, one large chicken wasn't appropriate. Edward searched the table for the salt, but it was still in the kitchen. She couldn't muster the social etiquette to tell him as much.

After several minutes of poking at her food, that beast of a man felt the need to strike up a conversation. "I imagine the couple is doing well."

"It seems that way. I admit I'm surprised Destiny hasn't come running back."

"She's stronger than you thought."

"No thanks to you," Helicant said, scraping her fork across the plate.

Edward chewed on a bite of chicken deliberately. "If I had known..."

"You'd what?" Helicant bit. "Be her father? She had a father, and he nearly killed her."

"I wouldn't have allowed that," Edward said.

"William had it in his head that the mainland would have doctoring facilities capable of caring for her. I wonder where he got such notions."

Edward's lip twitched. "I knew it was you; I didn't tell a soul."

No... He had no reason to.

William was insistent that Destiny could be cured somewhere else. He was not an idiot, her husband. If he believed such a thing, it was because someone of greater knowledge than him had said as much.

Only Helicant knew the island wouldn't let them leave, but Edward knew William was desperate enough to try.

Any interest Helicant had in eating was gone. She straightened in her seat and glowered at Edward. "No," she said, "Not when you could hold it over my head every night in bed."

Edward had eaten everything on his plate. He feigned stupidity at her comment, but before he could reply, the cart rolled up with rolls and several other foods. "There are the rolls!"

He brought the dishes to the table before hacking the chicken in half with the knife, taking the chicken breast, bone and all, to his plate. Helicant watched in disgust as greasy chicken liquid became trapped in his now fully formed beard. The chicken was still in his mouth when he grabbed several rolls and a slab of butter.

Sandwiching the two rolls together, he dropped the chicken from his mouth to stuff the rolls in its place. Helicant was repulsed by the display, but even more so that he thought he had some sort of claim on her daughter simply because he was the one who impregnated her.

"Honestly," Edward said. "I knew she was mine when I learned you were with child. William was so angry that you refused to let me monitor your pregnancy. I knew then it was mine."

"Because I couldn't stand the thought of you touching me again?"

Edward scowled at her and ate the leg she specifically asked him to reserve for Destiny. "Yes, because we parted on bad terms."

"William should have known as well," Helicant said with a fold of her arms. "We never engaged in marital acts."

Edward's brow furrowed. "I don't know if he was suspicious at all. Then again, maybe he didn't care how the child was conceived."

"I think most on this island are aware that you've been up nearly every skirt on this island. If William wanted to know who the father was, he need not look all that far."

"That's not fair, Helicant," Edward said over the bowl of potatoes. "I only pursued others when you rebuked me."

Helicant couldn't watch him stuff his mouth any longer. She knocked his plate off the table. He let out a growl but otherwise kept himself in check. "You cheat on my sister."

"Only with you."

Helicant didn't believe him. "And Abigail?"

Edward shook his head. "I've never touched Abigail."

This information set her on her heels, but his actions were still unforgivable. She stood up, pushing the chair out from under her, and got another glass of water from the pitcher.

"What we did was wrong," Helicant said. "It was wrong of me to take my sister's husband as a lover."

Edward seemed to have no remorse. He simply chomped away on a carrot with his fingers instead of a fork and knife. "Do you not care about how it hurt Beth?"

"I never meant to hurt your sister," Edward said softly. "I only agreed to marry her to get your attention. When you married William instead, I wanted to get back at you."

Still clutching the silver pitcher, Helicant turned to Edward, seething with anger. How dare he use Beth to hurt her. "Is that why you beat her?"

Edward stopped eating. It seemed the conversation made him lose his appetite. "How did you find out?"

Helicant scoffed. "There have been far too many times where my overtly social sister refused to see anyone. She's afraid of you. Drew hates you. I didn't need anyone to tell me; I know a beat dog when I see one." Helicant's voice was loud and shrill. "How dare you touch my sister? How dare you hurt her? If anyone killed her, it was you."

Edward shook his head. "No, it was just the few times. It wasn't intentional. I was drunk, and she was relentless."

"Some good doctor you are."

"It wasn't like that. Those nights were the worst of my life. I'd take it back if I could. Beth was so difficult sometimes."

"And you thought I'd let you in our lives?" Helicant took her place back at the head of the dining room. "That I would allow a raging, abusive drunk around Destiny?"

"If I were with you–with both of you, I would've been different."

"If Beth didn't talk so much, if you didn't drink so much, or if things were different, you would be different. But they're not, and you're not. We lead our lives with our actions, and your actions have spoken to me on numerous occasions."

Edward was pacing the room now. Scowling and stretching out his hands with their matted hair and unruly claws. "You're just a beast, Edward. Nothing more."

Sophie screamed from downstairs, but the good doctor deemed it unworthy of his attention. Edward sputtered and cursed under his breath before asking, "So your promise is false?"

"About Drew?" Helicant said. "No. Bring Drew to me instead of Destiny, and I will be with you."

"Forever?" He growled.

Helicant's fingers traced over her collar and down her chest, "Forever."

Edward ran from the room, leaving Helicant smiling. He would bring Drew to her, and she would make sure that boy never harmed Destiny again. Her daughter would carry on with her husband safely and happily. She'd suffer Destiny's anger even if it meant removing a threat to her only daughter.

Another shout came from the kitchen, and Helicant let out an exasperated sigh. "What is it now?" she grumbled, getting out of her chair.

Whoever released the scream was no longer in the kitchen. The only person to be found was Sophie in a state that brought Helicant to her knees. Her only remaining sister was hanging from the door of the dumbbell waiter.

The door must've slid shut on her elbows while she was placing something inside the device. The damned rolls. Sophie had been bleeding from where the doors shut, but the blood had dried and caked. The skin was torn around where the door landed, as if she had struggled to free herself before giving up.

Helicant vomited up the potatoes and beans she had eaten for Edward's sake. Sophie was dead. She had bled out all over the front of her dress.

How could all of this happen over the course of a few minutes? They heard her scream from downstairs not even fifteen minutes ago. She couldn't have bled out this quickly. Helicant kissed her sweet sister's face. It was cold and unyielding, nothing at all like Sophie.

She pulled the door to the dumbbell waiter up, allowing Sophie's body to slump to the floor. Her mangled arms came with—attached by some ligaments or muscle. Cradling her sister's body, Helicant rocked her like she did when she was a little girl with her baby sister. "What were you trying to do, you silly girl? You always try to take on more than you can manage."

There were no words for her loss. They were her sisters, but they were also her children. Helicant watched them grow and become their own people with their own dreams and ambitions, only to go like this? She couldn't allow it.

Something deep inside whispered words she couldn't understand. A song from lands she had never seen. A connection to something with the power to change what couldn't be changed otherwise. Helicant closed her eyes and gave herself to the chant. It soothed her aching head and replenished her withered soul.

Rocking back and forth with the song, Helicant understood and knew what she had to do. Not just for her sake but for Destiny's. This night was far from over. These sacrifices were all a part of something bigger.

The curse that gripped the island was coming undone.

Sophie wouldn't complain as Helicant bit into her dead flesh. Though the body was dead, the meat was still fresh enough to consume. Blood, the sweet essence of mortal existence covered, every layer of tissue and every morsel of fat. Helicant ate away at the arm, tearing away the dress with her teeth as she went.

The desire for meat only grew as Helicant ate. Insatiable and nagging. The chant in her mind had silenced, as did her grief and sorrow. There was nothing but her and her prey in that moment. It was only when she felt a clumsy hand swipe at her head that she stopped eating to look up.

A short, squat little lump of thick skin and leathery wings. After several lifetimes of failing, this night was unraveling in the most unexpected ways. She should've seen the signs earlier. The bird at the window and the hastened changes in her family. Helicant was afraid to hope, but the Cannibal was not.

"You're finally awake," she told the creature. "That's good. We've got work to do."

Destiny

"Walking with you is nice," Destiny said. It came out so awkward and wasn't what she meant. Even in the darkness of the night, he could probably still see her blushing.

"I can't see your eyes with how dark it is," she explained. "I feel like a normal girl."

"You are a normal girl."

With him, she really did feel that way. Well, as normal as things could be, given the situation.

"And nothing is normal about this," Daniel said. "We're out here in the middle of the night because we were hiding from our cousin who wanted to rape you. Edward was supposed to send us a sign, and he never did. Where is everyone?"

Destiny didn't have an answer for him. She was so used to her mother fussing over her all the time. "It is strange, but Mother told me things would change once I put the ring on. I just didn't think it would be like this."

Daniel paused to stare at the valley below them. The fog was so dense they couldn't see the ground. "It's like we're all alone on the island."

"Wouldn't that be wonderful?" Destiny said.

Daniel laughed. "You'd get tired of me if that were the case."

Destiny took his hand and gripped it tight. She got the urge to kiss him then. Leaning in, she lost her nerve, but she was so close that she couldn't back out. Daniel turned at just the right moment, and his lips met hers.

A little flick of electricity sparked, and Destiny gave a silent laugh with delight. Daniel cast his eyes downward in embarrassment. "Tell me another story," she said.

"I can't remember word for word."

"That's fine."

"The Jaw-Maul was one of the first monsters the Sallows family encountered on the island. It could run at great speed on all fours and made hideous noises on account of its facial deformity. The jaw was disconnected from the face, and the tongue dragged on the ground. It was attracted to noise, so it kept going after people when they were building the house."

Destiny wrapped herself tighter in the shawl she found at Sophie's. "Sounds so gross."

"They likened it to a hysterical woman. It would run at them, tearing at their faces and clothes while it desperately wailed for something they couldn't understand. It killed a child and several livestock. They had to reinforce the door to the catacombs to keep it inside."

The idea gave Destiny the chills. "Still not as bad as the broken one."

Daniel nodded. "Yeah, that one was bizarre. Just a broken body healed over and over. Its only ambition was to break the bones of others."

"But why?" Destiny asked. "Why would anything want their bones to break and heal wrong just to break it again? I can't understand."

"That's the point of monsters," Daniel explained. "We don't understand them, so they must be crazed beasts. Monsters represent what we don't understand and how it scares us."

"Then why does the green-eyed monster scare me so?" She asked.

Daniel gave it a moment to consider. "I think it's a metaphor for loneliness. I don't think you're afraid of eye color; you're afraid of being alone. Or maybe you're afraid of not being there when you're needed."

"When I'm needed?"

"You say that in your dream that he begs you to stay and that you don't. I think you're afraid that you'll leave and be alone forever."

"But he's a monster," Destiny said. "How could I stay? It would probably kill me."

"You'd be safer but alone."

Destiny turned and grinned at Daniel. It took him a moment, but Daniel's eyes narrowed. "You clever girl."

"You understand now?" she asked.

"No."

Destiny laughed.

"Yes," Daniel agreed. "I understand. Something about facing your fear and proving that you are not going to allow a dream to define your life any longer."

"And why does that matter to me now?"

"Because the whole island has gone insane?" Daniel said.

"Because now, I have something at stake. I like you, Daniel. I think I even love you. When I look you in the eyes, I want to feel you, not a phobia."

Daniel was rendered speechless. Imagine being such an intelligent, well-read man being brought down by so few words. Destiny took his hand again and pulled him towards the house. "Come on."

She practically dragged Daniel through the backdoor of the kitchen and came to a skidding stop. Daniel nearly tripped on her and wrapped his arms around her waist to steady himself.

"What the hell?" they both asked at once.

The kitchen had blood all over the counter, part of the wall, and the floor. Like someone bled all over the place before being dragged away. "What do you think happened?" Daniel asked.

"Maybe someone cut themselves and fainted before Edward could see to their injury."

"It looks like they were taken into the entryway," Daniel agreed.

Stepping over the bloody stones, Destiny and Daniel followed the trail until there was no longer one. They stopped right at the staircase. "They must have brought the person upstairs," Daniel said.

So, upstairs they went.

Her mother's room remained mostly undisturbed save for a drawer in the nightstand. Destiny took a peak inside and saw nothing suspicious. Daniel was staring at all her mother's things on the vanity but locked his hands together so that he wouldn't be tempted to touch a lady's things.

"Your mother uses all of these?"

Destiny nodded. "She has all sorts of potions."

"Mother told me something funny about Helicant," he said. "She told me that your mother is much older than the twins."

"She is," Destiny said.

"That she remembered her great great grandparents."

Destiny shrugged. "She said her great great grandfather had wooden teeth and used to pull them out of his mouth to entertain her."

"How old was she when she had you?" Daniel asked.

Destiny didn't know how old exactly. Her mother didn't celebrate her birthday. She said it was nonsense and didn't want anyone to know such intimate facts about her. "Not sure," she said. "I just know that it was supposedly a miracle. She said that one of these potions gave her a longer life but that she didn't want to live too long, so she only took half and hid the rest among her beauty potions."

Daniel seemed concerned by the answer. "She told you these things? As an adult?"

"No, she told me as a child. She probably didn't think I'd remember."

"I think that sort of thing would stay with a person."

Destiny smirked and looked at the vials. "Shall we find out?"

Daniel stepped back nervously. "I don't think so."

"Oh, come on," Destiny teased. "Is everyone so frightened of my mother?"

"Yes," Daniel nodded. "Yes, I am. And I'm not ashamed of that."

Destiny plucked up one of the vials. It was a dark red with a pointy top. She took out the stopper and sniffed. "This one is her perfume. I know because I saw Beth give it to her, and it smells like her."

Setting it aside, she took a green jar and sniffed, "This one is one of her face creams."

"This one is..." She inspected the contents of an amber jar.

"I think that's blood," Daniel said as he struggled not to gag.

Destiny set both aside and inspected one in a clear vial that was being held in a small metal stand. It looked like nothing more than water. The top was unusual, not made of anything found on the island. It was brown and had a bunch of holes in it. Yielding but firm enough to fit and seal the bottle.

"What do you suppose this is made of?"

Daniel took the brown stopper in his hand and inspected it. "I've never seen anything like it. It's light and buoyant but somehow waterproof even with all those holes in it."

"And this vial is half-full," Destiny teased.

"Your mother is going to be enraged."

Destiny sniffed the vial. It didn't smell like anything she'd ever known. She offered it to Daniel to smell as well. He ran it by his nose and shook his head. "I have no idea."

Without another doubt, Destiny drank half the potion. It tasted like water. It was probably just water. She wanted to see Daniel sweat it out just a little. His vexed expression went from her to the vial before sighing. "At least you have indoor plumbing."

She wasn't about to tell him that the plumbing didn't work. It had never worked. All those tubes and pipes in the washrooms were just for show.

He took down the remaining liquid and frowned. "Was that just water?"

Destiny went to her mother's water pitcher, refilled the vial to where it was, and replaced all her mother's belongings. "We're immortal now. Let's find that monster."

The Chimera

The creator looked over their body over appraisingly. The cave was low-lit with dozens of mostly used candles. Remains of other things lay scattered everywhere in various stages of decomposition. They were the only successful one.

He rummaged around the cave with arms outstretched and feverish in his excitement. The man pulled out a great pair of antlers attached to the skull of some long-dead creature and pressed it into their skull. There was pain at first, but as the creator worked, the pain dissolved into nothingness.

"Nothing has ever stayed alive this long," the man regaled.

It wasn't life that remained inside them. It was anger and a will to survive that surpassed logic and reason. Once untied from the cross, they'd inflict pain and fear on anyone within reach. It was the only existence they knew or understood. The only life that mattered.

The creator stepped back and looked again at their body. He folded his arms over his chest and tilted his head as if he were judging them. "I think I've just about got it."

He unhung a giant fish from the wall that smelled of brine. "The biggest fish I've ever caught," he told them. "I think if anything deserves my trophy, it's you."

The creator undid his belt, wrapped it around their appendage, and tightened it until the flesh ripped. Pressure built within the blocked extremity until their eyesight faded. There was a series of whacks followed by the sound of string being pulled through skin.

"This is the absurdist thing I've ever done," he laughed. "If they're going to hang me, I might as well do the things I want to do first."

With that, the creator paused as if at a loss for what he had done before taking a great pair of shears in his hand. They did not know what to expect, but their body slumped off the cross and to the ground.

Freedom.

His hands trembled, and he was muttering quietly to himself as he scratched at his smooth face with bloody fingernails. The Chimera only observed and made no attempts to lift their alien limbs or move their grotesque head. The creator was blowing out candles in the furthest part of the cave. Would he abandon them?

Part of the Chimera wanted the creator to stay and attend to them, but other parts wanted to hurt him. There were fragments that wanted nothing at all, but those parts may have already been dead. Mostly, they wanted a nest. The cave would make for a sufficient home, but they were not strong enough to defend it from the man just yet.

They saw it before the creator did. He had only blown out the candles on one side of the room when they saw it coming for him. It was fast. It crawled directly toward the cave along the forest ground. Its lower teeth shoveled dirt and dead leaves into its mouth as it went.

The man turned on instinct alone and saw it coming. The creature wailed a garbled noise and ran at him headfirst. He let out a cry of surprise and horror but managed to grab the shears to defend himself.

Crawling along the forest floor, the creature scrambled up the cave wall at an angle and lunged at the man sideways. They both went tumbling to the ground before the man threw the creature off him and got into a defensive stance with his scissors in hand.

"What the fuck are you?" the man asked.

The monster scampered around the cave, throwing things as it tripped over its tongue. The man could only stare at it in amazement while occasionally waving his sheers in front of him. They couldn't care less who won the encounter, just so long as both the man and the monster left the cave for the Chimera.

They needed to nest. They wanted to build a home for themselves where they could always be safe and secure. They wanted to be rid of the human and the beast and exist alone in this life.

The Chimera opened its mouth and let out a roar that startled the man. He stumbled backward away from them. The monster seemed indifferent to the threat. If they wanted to keep the cave, they would need to defend it. The man would be easy enough to frighten away, but the monster may stand their ground.

They rose to their hooves and reared their horned head high before spreading out their small wings and letting out a secondary roar. This time, their one scale arm and their other clawed arm spread out as they postured for a fight.

The man fell backward and crawled away. "Not possible," he said. "That's not possible."

The monster shook its head wildly, and its tongue waggled as its protruding red eyes stared blankly before it, too, backed away. It shrank into the forest and out of sight. The Chimera refocused their sights to the man who was babbling hysterically about possibilities before running and screaming into the night. With their competition gone, the Chimera spun around several times before curling up in a cozy spot on the ground.

THE GARGOYLE

Many things the Gargoyle did see. He saw a couple walking to the cottage together. They almost saw the Gargoyle too, but he jumped away and slid down the cliffside. If it were not for the cavern landing, the Gargoyle would have sunk into the sea.

The cliffside cavern led to a murky puddle carved from a great worm. Its tunnels led throughout the island, but the Gargoyle came back to the big house using a tunnel that ended in a fountain. The maze made him scratch his dirty head in confusion. He did not know which way to go.

His wings could not go far, but they were enough that the Gargoyle could hop over the maze lines and come out the other side. He skipped along the outside of the house and found pretty red flowers. Climbing up the wall where the flowers grew, their thorns scratched and clawed at his hide. He flew to a rooftop of the big house.

From there, he found many rooftops where he could see everything happening. There were many rooms in the house, but the Gargoyle simply followed the lights and sounds as there were not many.

In one of the highest rooms, he watched a man and woman making love. At least, he thought that was what they were doing. It was only when he watched that he saw his own reflection in the mirror, and his face made a frown in the reflection.

No female would touch him the way she touched the man.

After they had sex, the couple fought. It ended with the man leaving, but then something strange happened. The man suddenly appeared and disappeared while attacking the woman. The Gargoyle wanted to help but was frightened. If the man could vanish, what else could he do?

The woman saw the Gargoyle then.

She shrieked and ran at his appearance. It startled him so badly to hear a woman make such a noise that he forgot he was hanging upside down. Letting go of the roof, the Gargoyle hit the ground with his head.

He sulked in the wet darkness about the woman who screamed at the sight of him. Pulling at the flowers and letting them drop on the ground. The Gargoyle ate one—just to be sure it wasn't tasty, but the rest he left to wither and die on the ground. If he had to be ugly, the flowers would be ugly, too.

The Gargoyle was curious about the man and followed him all the way to the shore. He had stompy boots and thick hair like the man, so maybe the woman wouldn't scream when she saw him.

Deciding he must learn all he could from the man, the Gargoyle followed behind at a safe distance. More than once, the man turned and looked around suspiciously as if he knew he were being followed. Lucky for the Gargoyle, he was so short and hunched and grey, he blended in with the fog.

It was a long walk down the hill to the shore. The man was in a hurry on an island where there was nowhere to go, so the Gargoyle let the man fade from view. Instead, he practiced standing upright without the use of his knuckles. His back was permanently hunched, which made man-walking hard.

He found the bad man at the shore. He was pulling a boat out from hiding in the bushes. The man was tall and fit, but the boat was big, and he struggled to get it to the water. Another noise got the Gargoyle's attention.

He turned away from the man and saw a plump woman bustling out of the cottage. She tripped and fell many times. Her shoulder was injured. The smell of something rotting drifted under his nose. It was a bad smell that shouldn't be moving.

A dead man was limping after the woman. No longer fussing with the boat, the bad man was moving towards the injured woman. Only the bad man didn't help the hurt woman; he hid until the dead thing wandered off.

The bad man didn't deserve to leave this place. While he was hiding behind rocks and away from the woman who hid in a shack, the Gargoyle punched a hole into the man's precious boat. If the hurt woman couldn't get away, neither could the bad man.

He hated confrontation, it made him hop on all fours and sent his useless wings to flutter, but the Gargoyle was faster than a dead man at least. Throwing rocks at a distance, he was able to get the dead man to leave the shack and stalk in his direction. He used his wings to gather more distance between himself and the rotting man and eventually came upon the big house once more.

The Gargoyle walked within the fog with his hands dragging along the grass. He thought about the woman again and wondered if she was still in the room. He still had learned nothing about the man or what made him so appealing. If anything, he was bad, cowardly, and not worthy of a woman's love. Why should she touch him but scream at the nice Gargoyle?

The Gargoyle suspected it had something to do with the boots or maybe the jacket.

Another scream made the Gargoyle bounce back in fear it startled him so. The woman he saw up the stairs was running from the house and into the maze. Once he recovered, the Gargoyle slowly made his way to the sound within an open door in the kitchen. A different woman was broken in the wall.

He didn't know what the woman was doing or how she got there, but she was badly injured. If he understood these devices, he might have been able to help. If the Gargoyle knew how to be a man, he could help, but all the man had shown him was how to be cowardly and cruel.

The woman's eyes rolled about in her head for a moment before they became fixed on him. She groaned and tried to struggle free. With her last bit of energy, the woman kicked out at him with a booted foot before going completely limp.

The Gargoyle waited for several minutes to see if the woman would move. He approached her and slapped her foot before jumping away. She did not move. With more confidence, the Gargoyle got closer, grabbed her foot, and shook it. The woman's foot was heavy and floppy.

Looking around before he got closer, the Gargoyle placed a scaly paw on the woman's shoulder and gave her a gentle shake. She didn't budge, and her body remained flaccid. What was wrong with her? It was as if she was asleep and would never wake up. What would happen if she didn't wake up? He surmised that bugs would crawl up her nose and ears. Things would eat her until she was gone.

The Gargoyle supposed that if the woman was not going to wake up, she wouldn't need her boots anymore. Her boots were not like the man's boots. They were small and had buttons. He tried to take them, but they wouldn't come off her feet. The Gargoyle would need a different kind of boots than the ones the woman was wearing.

He looked up from the boots and found a large, hairy man staring at him. His eyes were large and golden, and his dark hair nearly covered his entire face. His man clothes were ripping at the seams. Straightening at the sight of the Gargoyle, the hairy beast outstretched his clawed hands and let out a snarl. Fear gripped the Gargoyle, and he yelped as he scrambled outside, forgetting all about boots or his man walking.

The beast chased him around the back side of the house. The Gargoyle spread his wings and flew up the stone wall beside the house and flew onto the roof like he had before. The Gargoyle was safe and let out a defiant laugh to mock the beast that scared him so. The beast let out a howl and wasted no time in running off to pursue his next victim.

The boots might not be there anymore, but it was worth a second look.

Clamoring to the ground, paying no mind to the noise he made, the Gargoyle returned to the woman trapped in the wall and found two women. Long black hair shielded a face smeared in blood as she crunched the bones between her sharp teeth and let out a hiss.

"You're finally awake," she told him. "That's good. We've got work to do."

What work did the woman need him to do? Standing on his hind legs, the Gargoyle posed and postured for her. Unlike the screaming woman, this one smiled at him. She liked him.

She left the house and padded with bare feet into the night. Her hair blended in with the darkness and shielded her as she discarded her man clothes. She giggled and danced in the night air underneath the white light of the moon.

What kind of woman was this? He hesitated, uncertain of what to do.

"Come along, my winged friend," she called.

The Gargoyle let out a cry of excitement. But... What if she wasn't talking about him? Were there other winged things around the big house? She didn't look at him when she said it, but he wanted to follow her all the same.

The woman turned around and looked at him this time. "It's okay," she promised.

Reluctantly, the Gargoyle followed, but at a safe distance to not frighten the beautiful woman. Her face was different from the others. It was sharp in places like his was. She had pointy teeth like him, too.

"Come here," she said.

The Gargoyle's heart was full as he approached. Trap or not, he would be happy to be ensnared. He tried to impress her with his best man walk. She smiled and kneeled with her hands outstretched to greet him.

Her embrace was warm and soft. The Gargoyle let out a whimper, and she stroked the top of his head. "Shh."

In that moment, the woman was everything to him. Her acceptance came without man boots or hair. As she took his hand, the Gargoyle decided he would do whatever the woman wanted. He would do anything to make the woman smile.

Destiny

For once in her life, Destiny was not afraid of getting lost in the house. She liked to think it was because she was being proactive, but a nagging voice in the back of her mind said it was because Daniel was there. She was alone in her dreams. Her husband wasn't holding her hand through it all.

"Tell me about the other monster," Destiny said. She needed a distraction from the doubt that was circulating in her thoughts.

"Well, there is the Beast."

"He's the one carved on the mantle."

Daniel nodded. "He had the most kills next to dysentery. The family actually killed him and made him into a pelt to be passed down from generation to generation."

"Mother has a pelt on her bed," Destiny said absently, her mind still coming back to the idea that she wouldn't have been able to search the house without Daniel. Maybe she wasn't facing her fears but coming up with a new coping mechanism. She supposed it was better than being afraid of green eyes. It was progress, wasn't it?

"Your mother would," Daniel muttered. "There is the Worm."

"What?" Destiny laughed.

He pulled the book from his pocket and confirmed. "Yeah, The Worm. They found fresh water because of it, but it was also a bit of a nuisance. It was partially responsible for building the catacombs as well. The family used the creature's tunnels to build the catacombs by closing off selected channels. It moves underground, so Nathanial didn't have much to say on how it looked or what it did. Nathaniel wasn't very good at his job."

Destiny was beginning to agree. "Well, if there was a giant worm thing underground and a gargoyle still running around, we'd probably have seen it by now, right?"

"It's a small island," Daniel said, shoving the book back in his pocket. "We'd see signs of something."

If there were never monsters to begin with, that would mean that her dreams were just that. Not some haunting recognition of fate. Probably a result of brain damage from a childhood fever. "Why make such an elaborate lie, though?"

Daniel shrugged. "Maybe the Sallows had other secrets. I read somewhere that Nathaniel was a bastard. I would venture that the safest place for a son no one wanted would be on a distant island."

Destiny bundled herself up more in her shawl and said nothing more on the matter. The whole thing was conflicting. In one way, it meant that she would have a new understanding of her own mental health, but on the other, it meant that their entire life was a lie.

"If you found out the monsters were never real, would you still want to stay here?"

Daniel looked at her and realized she was shivering. He took off his jacket and set it over her shoulders. "It's the only home I've ever known."

She suddenly no longer worried about whether monsters were real or not. Placing a hand on his face, Destiny found Daniel's lips with her thumb. She closed her eyes and kissed him. It wasn't so strange to keep her eyes closed while kissing—everyone did that from what she saw.

Daniel pulled her in close and kissed her with an urgency that sent her head spinning. Destiny bowed her head to regain her footing. "I think this has been the greatest but weirdest day of my life."

"Me too," he whispered.

If she didn't break free, Destiny was uncertain of what she would do next. Daniel turned away as he allowed her to move out of his arms and further down the hall. Destiny put her hand on a side table and steadied herself. For a fleeting, terrifying moment, she realized she was wearing the dress she had on in her dream.

"What is it?" Daniel asked.

She took a deep breath and reminded herself that the monsters were not even real. That much of the diary was made up, and that she was only doing this to prove it to herself. Of course she was wearing a dress like this in her dream; it was how most Sallows dressed for special occasions.

"Tell me another monster story," she said. Destiny was in dire need of a distraction.

"There's only one left. The Chimera," he said. Destiny heard a rustling of pages as Daniel read out loud. "The Chimera is a mockery of the Gods' creations. One of the most horrifying and strangest monsters on the island. It's as if the creature were pieced together by some madman. Its horned skull emerges from the flesh around the face, and it has large bird wings. One human arm wields a bird talon, and the other arm is a great fish with razor-sharp fins and sharp jagged teeth where the hand should be.

"It sits on cow hooves, and its legs are bent and jointed like a bird. It guarded its cave fiercely, but we smoked it out and lassoed the creature and dragged it back to the catacombs. It was yet another pitiful monster demonized by the travelers who encountered this island before us. There is no doubt in my mind that if left alone, most of these creatures would never hurt anyone.

"I regret accepting this cursed island. Had we not come here, many would still be alive. It is a place where man becomes beast, and the abominations that live here only serve to demonstrate the failures of man. If my father truly wanted myself and my family wiped from existence, there was no better place to send us."

"But...the king sent them," Destiny said, straightening her posture.

Daniel said nothing. She turned to look at him and found him staring at the pages as if he thought more words would appear. "Maybe the king acted on a lord's behalf?"

"Maybe," Destiny agreed. "There's no way to be sure,"

The hallways all looked the same, and so did most of the rooms. That was why, when Daniel opened a door and proceeded by, she almost didn't look inside. Destiny noted that the room was weirdly small and odd-shaped in comparison to the rest of the rooms. They had almost turned around and proceeded down another hallway, except she noticed something different.

Pointing at the wall, she said, "Something is missing here."

Daniel appraised the room but said nothing.

"There has been a window at the end of every hallway we've encountered."

"Where do you think we are on the map?"

"From what we've seen, the hallway snakes around several times per hallway," Destiny said. "All the rooms save the rooms with apartments are the same size... All but this one."

They stepped into a room half the size of her bedroom. It had a large armoire on the same wall as the door and the bed on the opposite wall. Mostly unfurnished, just like most of the rooms, but this one was more barren than the rest.

"Just a bed and a closet in here. Not even a mattress."

Daniel tilted his head as if he were in confusion. "There's no window in this one."

Destiny didn't think anything strange about it. "Most of the rooms don't."

"Yeah, but," Daniel walked out of the room and into the next, "This one does. As does the next," he called from several rooms down. Daniel came trotting back in, and their eyes made contact briefly before he averted his sight. It didn't really bother her this time. Not in comparison to before.

"Why would all the rooms on this side of the hallway have windows except this one?"

Suddenly, Destiny became rather keen on leaving. She gulped back the fear that rose in the back of her throat and understood why his eyes no longer frightened her. Green eyes were not nearly as frightening as the room.

They were close.

The Beast

As he sniffed the cool night air, the Beast let out a howl only to hear it fade into nothing. He had no pack. Only the promises of a wild woman and the thrill of the chase to spur him on. There were so many scents in the night already that the Beast struggled to maintain focus. She wanted the man.

Resting on his back haunches, the Beast searched the air for the trail that belonged to the man. He smelled something dark and conflicted. It stood out from the other tracks on the island. Chasing the scent down the road, he came upon a scent most deliciously foul. The Beast couldn't help but stop to investigate the smell of rotting meat. It was so intense that it filled his mouth and made him salivate.

The lumbering body was making its way up the hill. The flesh was shriveled and black. It was a wonder that it could keep going. The Beast swiped at the body, tearing the arm right off with his claws, but the dead thing continued to walk. The dead thing was entirely unmoved by the loss of its arm. The Beast was tempted to pursue, but there was a whole arm waiting to be eaten.

The Beast ripped into the severed arm and gnashed the bones between his teeth. They were softer than bones ought to be, but the marrow came pouring out, and the Beast savored the flavor that was euphoria. With all traces of the arm gone, the Beast turned to chase after the dead thing but was stopped by the voice of the wild woman in his head.

"There's plenty of time for that later. First, bring me the man."

The Beast snapped at the air and let out a growl of frustration. He wanted the dead meat, but she promised to give him something important. If only he could remember what it was.

Refocused, the Beast followed the man's scent down to the water of salt and sand. The Beast didn't like water, so he avoided the tides that threatened to get him wet. There was the smell of wood and another creature's scent. The smell of another's blood lured him into a house where he could smell the dead thing.

Iron and sweat trailed into a shack, but there was no meat. He lapped up the blood and savored the flavors. It wasn't the man's blood, but he had to check just in case. The man's scent could be found again several yards up where he and the blood's owner moved together.

He wished he could remember what the wild woman promised him. Was it crunchy and scrumptious? Rotting and fleshy or fresh and firm? There was so much in the world the Beast wanted to eat. There was also rage. A deep-seated rage that made him roar at the night even when nothing would ever roar back at him.

The Beast followed the man's scent into the forest and into a cave. Only the smell of the woman was gone. The scent of blood overwhelmed the Beast, and he charged into the cave with little regard for the scent of something else that now resided in the cave.

A new kind of creature squalled at him and slashed at him with hooked claws. The Beast jumped back with a whimper. He looked at the thing and thought about taking it on. He bared his teeth and squared his feet, ready to strike.

"Find the man," the wild woman's voice boomed in the cave.

Both the Beast and the other creature ducked in alarm before the Beast was off and running. Through the forest where the trees and moss grew. Where leaves and sticks crunched underfoot and where the wild things belonged.

Emerging from the forest, the Beast paused to sniff the air. The man had altered his course, and the Beast was uncertain of which way his prey had gone. It was as if the man knew he was being followed and acted accordingly.

The Beast ran in the direction of the smaller house closer to the forest. The man had gone there for certain. The fog gave way as he strode through the short green grass. Livestock panicked as they sensed his presence.

The smell of their fear and their flesh became overwhelming for the Beast. He knew the woman would be angry, but he couldn't resist ripping into the pigs and chickens. Basking in the glow of the massacre he had created, the Beast did not notice the scent of the man was concentrated nearby.

A loud popping noise followed by searing pain in his shoulder, the Beast reared back with his bloody claws and howled in agony. Something felt as though it were burning into him, leaving a gripping pain in his chest.

The man was in the house and had a metal tube that shot fire in his hands. He let out a roar and charged the window, but the man picked up a different fire stick and took aim.

Another exploding noise and the fire burned into the Beast's heart. He fell to his knees and yowled. He pleaded for the wild woman to come to his aid. She was in the air, and he knew she had seen what the man had done to him, but no aid came from the woman.

The Beast fell to the ground unconscious while the man let out a shout of triumph. He heard another shot, but where the fire went this time, the Beast couldn't say.

He had failed her again.

The Worm

While the monsters lurked in dark rooms, shallow caves, and inside houses, the Worm operated within a labyrinth of channels within the marrow of the island itself. It was a freedom seldom few understood. When the little winged goblin flew into their cave, the Worm allowed his trespass. He was a silly, harmless thing, after all.

After being asleep for so long, the Worm worked her many tentacles throughout the island, feeling for information. There was so much to learn. Humans and monsters alike were roaming the island. The witch was among them. She scrapped along the caverns with seething dislike.

If she wanted to reproduce this time, she would need to find a way to do it without the witch finding out. The witch always found a way to kill her offspring. The Worm flexed with anger as it stretched and found new purchase in the soil. Despite having access to nearly every part of the island, the witch remained elusive.

There was the sound of several pops before a single pair of footprints thumped along the surface. A single victor emerged, and he was proudly walking toward the largest building on the island. The reverberations were most likely human, and humans made the perfect hosts for her children.

Her tendrils detected more humans inside the house. Two of them. They were walking inside the building without any sense of urgency. She supposed these humans could serve as well. The Worm worked her finer tendrils through the copper tubes closest to the pair. Tips tasting air, the humans were close, but they were still too large for the pipes within the house.

The Worm squeezed and wedged herself further through the pipes until the pipe burst from the wall and came falling to the floor. Not wanting to be seen, she squeezed back into the pipe and away from open air.

"What was that?" A female voice asked.

"I'd rather not find out," said the man.

Footsteps came into the room. "The pipes in the bathroom have just imploded?" the man said, picking up the pipe the Worm had just inhabited.

"That's strange," the woman said. "Nothing flows through them."

Snaking her way back out of the room and into the next, she would have several tendrils ready and waiting. With one section in the building, the Worm navigated the burrows under the forests and another around the cottage closest to the shore.

The Worm sought for signs of the witch. She wasn't in the house or in the cliffside cottage. It wasn't long before her strands felt the drumming of feet. Rhythmic and ancient as the dance formed a circle. It was her; it had to have been.

The witch was far enough from the mansion with all the remaining humans, she let the appendage in the forest go lax. She'd know the moment the dance stopped. Meanwhile, her tendrils in the house took to another room. It was similar to the others with piping. The Worm pushed through the pressure of the confining plumbing until their larger, more primary arms could get through.

The pipes groaned in protest until they finally tore and gave way to her scaled and sucker arm. Underneath the impenetrable skin was a dense muscle that could break rocks if she squeezed hard enough. To prove her own point, the Worm slapped at something hard and delighted as it shattered like glass.

The Worm searched the room for a way out. She could hear the voices of the humans on the other side of a wall but couldn't figure out how to reach them. There had to be a way in the room since the humans did it all the time, but it was beyond her. She felt something hard and round against a grooved portion of the wall. It gave fractions of an inch when she pressed against it, but it was a mystery as to how it worked.

The voices remained on one side several feet away. She had an intimate understanding of the building, and they knew that each wing had four hallways, except for on this level, there were five. Navigating through a house's plumbing gave her this understanding, even if the humans were unaware of the anomaly.

There hadn't been any noises or vibrations in the fifth hallway for a long time. Perhaps the humans couldn't figure out how to get inside anymore. That would put a damper on her plan.

There also remained the pesky fact that she could not find a way out of the room. Frustration mounted as the Worm coiled around the furniture and other items in the room. Things crunched and groaned with the weight of her limbs pooling within the secret room.

It wasn't like she could suck them all back in at once. She had no choice but to wait until her tendrils slowed on their own before reversing course or breaking through the walls that separated them from the goal of a lifetime.

Abandoning the search for an exit, the Worm pressed against the wall. She could feel the structure protesting. Beams resisted, but the thin wood that served as the walls splintered and gave way.

The humans screamed and ducked to a corner as the Worm's arm punched through the wall that separated them. In a moment, the Worm thought she was successful, but by the time the other limbs reported back to their brain, it was too late.

Sharp nails raked against their scales, severing limbs and forcing her to retreat.

The witch had stopped dancing ten minutes ago, but the Worm was too preoccupied to notice. She let out a scream and reeled away as the witch attacked. Liquid spilled from the wounds and stumps as she sought reprieve.

Desperation had kicked in. Yes, the limb was no longer exposed, but it was now useless and would only slow them down. The Worm could always regrow a new one, but she had little option when it came to human hosts.

Without sentiment, the Worm jerked the injured extremity around its tunnels in quick, snapping motions. It was enough to break free of the deadweight, but the witch had once again disappeared.

The Cannibal

The flesh was not the freshest, but when she bit into the shoulder, years were returned to her. Ripping off a chunk, the Cannibal chewed in a half grin as she came to a new understanding about who she was and the life she lived up until this point.

Unlike everyone else on this island, she could remember who she was and why this was all happening. They were becoming their true selves once more. All she had to do was make sure Destiny opened the door.

A hand weakly grasped hers. The Cannibal looked down to see that the Bone-Breaker had finally awoken. To the human eye, she would've appeared to be the woman named Sophie, but as a witch, she knew better.

She dropped the creature and broke the hand that gripped hers. It let out a groan and writhed in a way that could only be described as sexual in nature. The Cannibal let out a sigh of disgust and clamped her hand on the monster's throat.

"Bizarre creature," she said as she clamped the throat shut, breaking the neck. "Won't be making those noises anymore."

The Bone-Breaker's neck was snapped. Bones protruded from its neck, bent to one side. The Cannibal watched for several minutes as the creature convulsed and wondered if she had made a mistake. The light in the creature's eyes was growing dim.

"Perhaps it was too soon." She said, kneeling to have a better look. Her black hair cascaded in curtains on each side of her petite face.

The Bone-Breaker jolted to life, only its face seemed to be permanently discolored. It writhed and croaked with its arms outstretched to her, begging for more pain. With equal amounts of disgust and pity, the witch lifted the creature off the ground with a hand around the neck and walked it to the basement stairs, where she let go.

"That should do the trick."

The Bone-Breaker rolled down the stairs, several of its bones snapping along the way. The body broke through the railing at the platform of the steps before falling into a heap on the floor. The Cannibal folded her arms, leaned against the doorframe, and watched as the Bone-Breaker got back up—its bones healed exactly where they broke.

Their thighbone now protruded through the skin, giving the dress a strange lift at the side. The arms had healed in different positions; one elbow now went in the opposite direction while the other had regrown to the side. The small neck bones remained where she had broken them, but now the head jutted back weirdly.

"You must have smacked your head on the way down."

The Bone-Breaker also had a foot on backward. The Cannibal watched as it shambled its way up the steps once more. She tapped her foot as the thing took its time. She had many things to do, and it was all up to her to make it happen.

Finally, the thing reached the top of the steps beside her, where it looked deeply into her eyes before extending a hand. It was inviting her to join it. To share its pain because, to this creature, pain was the ultimate pleasure.

Rolling her eyes, the Cannibal let out a long breath and said. "Just once. I'm a busy woman."

Hand in hand, the two monsters flung themselves down the narrow staircase. Their skulls collided at least once, and the Cannibal felt her hip as well as an arm break before she collapsed at the landing. The Bone-Breaker rolled down the remaining steps and rolled into the darkness.

Sitting up, the witch reset her broken arm, hip, ribs, and several fingers. Everything else seemed intact. Fortunately, the Bone-Breaker had suffered a great deal more. Her face had been smashed in at several points, and her nose was almost completely shoved into her skull. Her body was bent and broken in ways that were impossible to comprehend.

"Bone-Breaker," the Cannibal said. "There you are at last!"

Skipping down the steps like a young girl, the Cannibal kissed the monster's head, which was no longer the top of the misshapen thing, and proceeded up the steps.

"I've got to go now. Have a good night."

The Cannibal inhaled the night air and noted the hints of mongrel blood. He failed her in killing Drew. He always failed her in the end. She wouldn't let it bother her. This time, things would be different. Destiny was different this time; the witch could sense it, though she wasn't certain what changed in the girl. Perhaps she was tired of being murdered night after night.

Gentle scrapping noises came from the rooftops, and the Cannibal smiled. "Come on, now."

Her little but most loyal friend flew down from the rooftops. He didn't remember her—how could he? Poor thing was frightened and so sad. At least this time, she didn't find him marching around in human clothes. Such acts were beneath him. The Gargoyle followed her into the woods, occasionally letting out a screech of excitement.

"Have you seen the Jaw-Maul lately?" She asked.

The Gargoyle only tilted its head while its wings ruffled.

"That must mean no. Come. If we start a commotion, they will surely come."

The trees sung in the night air as the moon glared down at them. The witch observed that the man on the moon was no longer there. She wondered how he had escaped that desolate rock. He had been there for as long as she remembered.

"If he could find a way out, so can I," she said.

The Gargoyle had no idea what she was saying, but she kissed his forehead, and he jumped up and down before spinning around with joy.

"I'll find a way for all of us to get off this island."

They came to a clearing in the wood, and the witch pinched a bit of soil and tasted it. "This is a good place for a fire," she declared.

The Gargoyle wasted no time gathering wood to stack into a pile. The Cannibal closed her eyes and lifted her arms to the sky as she swayed her body to the sound of the forest. So much of herself had been trapped inside a woman who had lived far too long. A woman who did not dance or enjoy tearing flesh from bone with her teeth.

It was like living inside a nightmare.

With the wood piled high enough, the witch turned and flung another pinch of dry dirt on the kindling, and a fire rushed to life nearly six feet tall. The Gargoyle jumped and screamed with delight, and the Cannibal laughed with relief. Her powers were truly there, and she was not an old woman living in captivity.

"Dance with me," she said to the Gargoyle. Together, they spun around the roaring fire, dancing in whatever way pleased them. Shaking off the mortal skins, they released their call into the night, waiting to see who all might come.

She could feel the Jaw-Maul rushing towards her. It was a violin string being plucked. A pitch that only dogs could hear. They were racing toward her, but in that moment, the earth shifted underneath the Cannibal's feet, and she realized something else was also coming.

"Stay here. I need to take care of something."

Not wanting to be detected, the Cannibal scaled a tree and moved along their branches. The Worm had also woken. She flung herself from the last tree in the forest towards the house. Calling to the wind, a strong gust guided her to the rooftop of the mansion where the Cannibal's worst fear was coming to pass.

The Worm was attacking Destiny.

Her heart pounded as she scaled over the roofs and plunged feet first through a glass window. The Beast would not have Destiny. She was not for this world. Destiny did not belong to the monsters. The witch's claws tore through armored scales as she lunged at the creature with all her might.

The Worm recoiled and forced itself back through the pipes from whence it came, damaging itself to escape. The Cannibal wiped her face and stood in smug satisfaction. How dare that creature go near her daughter? It was likely she did not know who she was attacking, but the Worm could not be allowed to reproduce in any case. The balance of the world relied on that.

She couldn't kill it, but she could kill all the humans that remained on the island—save Destiny—of course. That was where the Jaw-Maul came into play. There was also a Zombie on the island, but it was a useless thing. The Cannibal couldn't manipulate something with rot for brains.

A spine-chilling wail rolled over the island, and the Cannibal smiled. It seemed the Jaw-Maul would come to her. She stepped off the roof and landed gently on the ground. There, the witch waited as the scurrying noises announced the monster's presence.

"What a hideous thing you are," she said to the deformed figure. Its tongue dragged on the ground as it crawled on haunches and palms. Red eyes shone at her even in the dim light of the twilight.

"I need you to find the human. Find him and keep tabs on him. Keep him running, keep him afraid. It's fine if you accidentally kill him; just do not let the Worm get to him. I'm relying on you."

The Jaw-Maul let out a cry and crawled off in pursuit of the man. The Cannibal took a deep breath and said. "It's almost time."

Destiny

"Are you okay?" Daniel asked, shaking the debris out of his hair.

Destiny was wide-eyed and shaken, but she didn't think she was hurt. She nodded as she dusted off her dress. "I think so."

"Stay here, I'm going to take a look."

Destiny didn't want him to go. She wanted to turn right back around and forget any of this happened. Daniel's curiosity peaked, and there was no stopping him from investigating the enormous hole in the wall or what had caused it.

"I want to go now," she told him with a shaky voice.

"Daniel," she called.

There was no answer. She didn't want to go in there after him, so she waited for him to come back to her.

Several minutes had passed. Destiny called for him again and again, but there was no answer. She was starting to feel frantic. Pacing around, Destiny shook her hands out as she struggled to cope. She couldn't stand to be alone. Daniel wasn't supposed to leave her like this. She whimpered as she sucked in shallow breaths, wondering what she was going to do.

She let out a cry of frustration and made her way back to the stairway. Destiny would find someone to come and help her find him. She took off in a full sprint, lifting her dress as she ran only to stop—her face less than an inch away from a face she hadn't seen before.

Destiny gasped and swung her arms out to keep balance. The girl before her looked wrong somehow. Her face was like a caricature of a human face. Like a mask hiding something more sinister behind it. Her black eyes and black hair only made the sheet-white skin more unnatural.

"Who are you?" Destiny stuttered.

"I'm here to help," the girlish voice promised.

"I've never seen you before. Did you come from the mainland?"

The girl took Destiny's hand and said, "You look frightened."

She swallowed and said, "Yes, I lost my friend Daniel, and I'm worried about him."

"I'll help you find him."

Destiny found the girl's presence to be soothing as it was confusing. It sparked so many questions in her mind. Perhaps the reason why she and Daniel didn't see anyone is because mainlanders came to shore. Nothing like that had happened before, but it made sense. Everyone would go rushing to the new arrivals, forgetting all about them.

At the same time, something was strangely familiar about the girl. It was like she had always known her... But that was impossible. Destiny struggled to remember who the youngest person on the island was, but it made her head hurt, and she realized she couldn't remember. But she did know that it wasn't this girl.

"Everything seems so fuzzy."

"I imagine so," the girl said. "You've only repeated this situation hundreds of times. Each time with slight deviations. At this rate, you probably can no longer differentiate between dream and reality when you step through that threshold."

Destiny screwed up her face and looked at the girl. She looked like a young girl but spoke like an old woman. "What are you talking about?"

"Your dreams were memories."

Destiny shook her head from left to right; she felt like she did when she drank the punch Drew gave her. The girl was gone, but she still felt the warmth of a hand in hers. What had the girl done to her? What did all this mean?

"Daniel?" She cried out.

"He needs your help," the girl said.

Destiny heard someone pounding on a door and yelling. It was Daniel. He was trapped and needed her. "It was never a dream?"

"No," the girl explained. "You're not crazy, and this has happened many times. Each time, you've chosen to run away because you were scared. Because you were alone. This time is different. I am here with you."

"Daniel is behind the door, isn't he?"

"Long have we been cursed to remain on this island. The only way to break it is for you to open the door. If you do not, it will start all over again."

"What will happen to me?" Destiny whispered, clutching her hand to her heart. "I don't understand."

"Time is like a ring," the girl explained. "It goes around and around. Sometimes, a ring becomes warped or dented. You, my dear, are that dent. My impossible child. Somehow, you were born new and clean of the curse. Though the island still means to trap you, make you live out this critical point in time day after day. Open the door and set us free."

"Mother?" Destiny was intoxicated by her perfume and her voice. She was no longer in the room, but she could be felt everywhere.

"Go to him, my love," her mother said. "Go to him so that you can be free to live."

Destiny shook her head and leaned against the nearest wall. She stared at the peeling wallpaper and took several slow, deep breaths before she allowed herself to think about anything she had just heard.

What if she never escaped from Drew? She could feel him slinging her incapacitated body over his shoulder as he took her into the woods. Her body was cold when he left her there. They wouldn't find her corpse until after the winter snows had melted, and only her bones would remain.

What if the fever she had as a child had killed her? Destiny could feel her body burning up as she lost herself in feverish delusions and chills broke out throughout her body. Edward was unable to save her, and her mother never forgave him of that.

She wasn't crazy. Those were all things that happened, and her mind struggled to reconcile with it. It came out as a dream that she was irrationally afraid of—not able to understand what it really was.

Muffled screaming and crying jolted Destiny's thoughts, and her sights narrowed toward the end of the hallway. He was so afraid. Destiny ran at the door, not wanting to waste any more time. Mostly because she was afraid to hesitate.

Destiny pressed herself against the door while Daniel raged on the other side. She looked through the peephole and felt as though the wind had been knocked out of her. Soft, jovial Daniel had shed his baby weight and was now nearly emaciated. His sharp cheekbones and broken expression made him almost unrecognizable.

He was pleading with her to open the door. Daniel knew she was looking at him. He was naked from the waist up, and there wasn't a bit of skin that wasn't shredded or bruised.

"Why won't I die?" he shouted.

Destiny realized that time didn't work in that room. What was only a half-hour for her was a lifetime for him. He had been suffering for such a long time. Daniel wept and said her name before shouting in anger.

"Why won't you open the door? You know I'm here!"

His rage frightened her. She stepped away from the door and was about to bolt when she picked up the scent of her mother's perfume and remembered what she came here for. She needed to open the door.

She closed her eyes and turned the knob.

THE CANNIBAL

She found no sign of anyone outside the manor. This alarmed the witch greatly, as she was relying on her fellow monsters to keep the Worm from finding the man. She had set Destiny up for her task; the rest was up to her daughter.

The Cannibal let out a sigh. Of course the survival of the world as anyone knew it relied on her. Closing her eyes, the witch focused her power on finding the human. Arms outstretched, her fingers searched the air as if they combed the grounds of the island itself.

Her black eyes flew open. "The basement."

Rushing into the kitchen and down the stairs, she found the Worm had broken through the door to the catacombs and had Drew in their tendrils. She hissed and lunged at the creature while the pathetic boy pleaded and cried.

She tore at the extremities, but the Worm had the man in her grasp and was pulling him into the catacombs. The Cannibal was in a panic. If the Worm took Drew, her only choice would be to stop Destiny from opening the door.

If the door remained shut, the time loop would start over, giving her another chance, but what if she was too late?

The Worm wasted no time in doing their work. A small tendril worked up the man's pant leg and penetrated. He let out an enraged scream as the Worm pumped their offspring into his warm body. There, they would attach to one of his organs and hatch. After devouring the body, thousands of worms would create deeper, longer tunnels to seek out new hosts. The world would collapse in on itself from these massive worm tunnels as countless worms inseminated who knows how many humans.

The Cannibal shredded at the extension coming from the basement, but it was too large and too strong. It was a major artery and nearly impossible to fight. The witch let out a scream of rage and tore harder with her claws when something thudded down the stairs.

She ignored the noise and opted to tear off the insemination tendril along with anything else in the basement now filled with the Worm. The man let out a gargled scream, and the Cannibal smelled blood. Bolting upright, she turned around to find the Zombie had climbed over the Worm's limbs and was chewing on the man's neck.

The Worm acknowledged its loss and loosened its grip on the man. The man slumped to the floor as the mass of Worm slithered back into the catacombs. The Zombie ravaged the still-twitching body as it leaked out shit and slime. She noted the human had a raging erection but decided it wasn't worth a second thought.

With the Worm defeated and Destiny at the right place at the right time, the Cannibal unleashed one final spell. She dispelled the old woman's perfume around Destiny to give her a reminder that she was never alone.

The air around her contracted. Her pupils dilated, and something like the scent of the first day of spring came wafting through the cellar.

Something had fundamentally shifted. It could've been the Worm retreating, but she didn't think so. This was the quiet in the moments before a babe took their first breath. A faun walking on wobbly legs. An exhausted hatchling breaking free of its egg.

"Destiny…"

***

The sun rose to the first new day for the first time in over six hundred years. The witch watched the sun rise over the ocean and fell to her knees as she sobbed. Destiny had opened the door. All the monsters were free—all but the Worm, who had overgrown its tunnels and would be unable to leave this cursed place.

Beside her, the Gargoyle looked up at her as if to ask, "What do we do now?"

"I don't know," she said. "I always planned our escape, not for what we would do when it finally happened."

The fog was moving off the island and away into the distant oceans. Several boats were in the bay. No doubt they were confused about the island that suddenly appeared before them. She would be leaving in one of those boats; that much was certain.

The Gargoyle screeched and pointed at the house.

"What happened to Daniel and Destiny?" she said for him. "They can leave the room whenever they like. I imagine they are honeymooning."

Men huddled together in groups as they walked the shores of the island. The Cannibal's belly growled. These were plump men. Skinny men, too. Even a woman treaded along the shore. Her blood went hot, and she smiled a thin smile. There would be no trace left.